CW01637611

Wrapped Up

A Silk tie, a spicy confession: One woman's Christmas journey from cynicism to ecstasy

"Ecstasy & Enchantment" holiday romance series

Marlyn Love

Foreword

"Buckle up, girl - you're about to discover that a little Christmas magic can lead to a whole lot of sensual ecstasy. Don't say I didn't warn you..."

Chapter 1

Jennifer

L*ove is a fickle, cruel mistress.*

I scoff, scanning the crowded dance floor. Couples sway to the pulsing beat, bathed in the club's dim, flickering lights.

"You know, I'm pretty sure they put something in the air at these places," I mutter to Anna, who's perched beside me on a bar stool. "Some kind of chemical that just makes people want to latch onto the nearest warm body and never let go."

Anna spins around, her blue eyes sparkling with mischief under the flashing neon lights. "Oh, come on, Jenn! Don't be such a Grinch. This is the perfect place to find your own Christmas Prince." She wiggles her eyebrows suggestively, grinning as she gestures toward the dance floor.

I roll my eyes. "Anna, it's the end of November. Christmas is still a month away. The only thing I'm finding here is a headache and a one-way ticket to Heartbreak Hotel." I take a long sip of my drink, savoring the liquor's slow burn.

Anna gasps dramatically, pressing a hand to her chest as if I've mortally wounded her.

“Jennifer Marie Thompson! How dare you suggest that it's too early for Christmas? There's no such thing!”

I can't help but chuckle at her theatrics. “I forgot that I was talking to the Queen of Christmas herself. Remind me again, how many strings of lights did you put up last year? Five hundred? A thousand?”

“Two thousand, thank you very much,” she replies, tossing her hair. “And that’s not counting the inflatable Santa, the life-size reindeer, or the animatronic elves.”

I shake my head, amused despite myself. Anna's Christmas obsession is legendary in our circle of friends. Last year, her place looked like the North Pole had exploded inside it. I'm pretty sure she single-handedly kept the local power company in business during December.

“You know,” I tease, “I think I saw a store the other day that still had some Halloween decorations. Perhaps we should go back to those instead.”

Anna's eyes widen in horror. “Don't you dare! Jenn, Halloween is over! It's time for mistletoe, miracles, and finding your very own Christmas Prince!”

I laugh. Even in my cynical mood, I can't help but feel a surge of affection for her. Anna's enthusiasm for life, and especially for Christmas, is both exhausting and endearing.

“Alright, alright,” I concede, holding up my hands in mock surrender. “I bow to your superior Christmas spirit. Just promise me you won't try to set me up with another guy dressed as an elf. I'm still traumatized from last year's Christmas party.”

Anna's eyes twinkle mischievously. “No promises, my dear Grinch. No promises at all.”

Despite my cynicism, I can't help but feel a rush of

warmth for this bubbly blonde whirlwind who's been my rock since childhood. We're polar opposites, yet our friendship has weathered every storm life's thrown our way.

I watch as she scans the crowd, no doubt searching for my potential "Christmas Prince." Not surprising. Her brain's addled because she snagged the only perfect guy on the planet.

"Not everyone can be as lucky as you and Peter," I say, swirling the ice in my glass. "Some of us have to settle for less than ideal situations."

Anna's eyes soften, and she squeezes my hand. "You deserve more, Jenn. The right guy is out there. You just need to open your heart."

I snort, pulling my hand away. "Right. Because that worked out so well with Felix."

The name hangs between us, heavy with unspoken pain. Felix, the charming bastard who'd swept me off my feet, only to drop me unceremoniously when a newer, shinier model captured his attention.

Anna's face clouds, but she shakes it off. "Felix was a jerk. Not every guy is like him. Look at Peter!"

I can't help but smile. The way Peter adores Anna is disgustingly sweet, like a fairytale.

"Peter's one in a million, Anna. And you've already got him locked down." I drain my drink, signaling for another. "Some of us just don't fit the whole 'happily ever after' thing."

Anna opens her mouth, no doubt ready to argue, but I cut her off. "Anna, you know I love you, but please don't try to set me up with anyone tonight, okay?" I say, keeping my voice light. "I mean it. No more Mr. Wonderful or holiday-themed suitors, alright? I'm done with that scene. I just want to have a wonderful time with my best friend."

Anna pouts, but there's a determined glint in her eye that makes me nervous. “Fine, no more setups. But promise me you'll at least try to have fun tonight? Who knows, maybe your Christmas Prince is right around the corner.”

I roll my eyes, but I can't resist her puppy-dog expression. “Fine, I promise to have fun. However, if I find myself alone with a bottle of wine on New Year's Eve, don't judge me.”

I take another sip of my drink, letting the cool liquid distract me from Anna's relentless enthusiasm. As I lower my glass, my eyes drift across the crowded bar, scanning the sea of faces without really seeing them. Until suddenly, they land on a man standing on the other side of the bar, leaning casually against the polished wood. He's tall, broad-shouldered, with jet-black hair that's just messy enough to look effortlessly stylish. Even from here, there's an intensity in his gaze as he scans the room.

My breath catches in my throat, and a fluttering sensation fills the pit of my stomach. For a moment, I can't look away. He's undeniably attractive, the kind of man who commands attention without even trying. The kind of man I used to fall for, hook, line, and sinker.

The kind of man who always breaks my heart.

I force my gaze away, my fingers tightening around my glass. No. I won't go down that road again. I've been burned too many times, and it left me with nothing but ashes and regret. The last thing I need is another charming smile hiding a heart of ice.

But even as I try to focus on anything else, I can feel the phantom pull of his presence. It's ridiculous. I don't even know him. He could be a complete jerk, for all I know. He probably is, if my past dating patterns are any indication.

“Jenn!” Anna's voice cuts through my thoughts, bright and bubbly. “Come on, it's time to dance!”

Before I can protest, she's grabbing my hand, tugging me towards the crowded dance floor. I stumble, nearly spilling my drink.

"Anna, wait—"

Too late. The music thrums through me as we plunge into the mass of bodies.

My best friend twirls, her flowy bohemian dress swirling around her legs like a kaleidoscope of colors. She's a vision of carefree joy; her blonde hair catches the light as she throws her head back, laughing.

I glance down at my own outfit—a fitted black dress that hugs my curves, its neckline modest, hemline skimming just above my knees. A far cry from Anna's free-spirited ensemble, but it feels like me. I smirk, remembering Felix's critiques:

"You should show more skin," he'd say, his eyes roving over my body with barely concealed disappointment. "Dress sexier. You've got the body for it."

The memory stings, but I shove it aside. Tonight, I'd decided to embrace my femininity on my own terms. The dress is a little more form-fitting than my usual fare, the fabric clinging to my hips and waist in a way that makes me feel powerful rather than exposed.

Anna catches my eye and grins, grabbing my hands and spinning me around. "You look amazing, Jenn!" she shouts over the music. "That dress is killer! You're turning heads left and right."

I glance back towards the bar, involuntarily seeking out the stranger. Heat blooms in my cheeks as our gazes lock, and he smiles—slow and devastatingly sexy.

No. I wrench my eyes away, breaking the spell. I'm not doing this. I've been burned before, and I refuse to let another pretty face lead me into making the same mistakes.

The music shifts, a sultry rhythm taking over. Anna immediately grabs Peter, who had been chatting with a friend at the bar, and now he's watching us from the sidelines with an indulgent smile.

As Anna melts into Peter's arms, I feel a pang of longing deep in my chest. I squash it down, forcing a smile.

"I'm gonna hit the ladies' room," I shout over the music. "You two lovebirds enjoy yourselves."

Anna flashes me a concerned look, but I wave her off. I need a moment alone, away from the swaying couples and the pulsing beat that seems to mock my solitude.

I weave through the crowd, the heat of bodies pressing in on all sides. The air feels thick, heavy with perfume, sweat, and unfulfilled desires. As I reach the edge of the dance floor, my skin prickles with awareness, and I know without looking that the handsome stranger is still watching me. I quicken my pace, my heels clicking against the floor in a staccato rhythm that matches my racing pulse.

What is wrong with me? One look from a stranger rattle me like this. I'm stronger now. Smarter. I've learned my lesson about men with smoldering eyes and secret smiles.

I push open the bathroom door, grateful for the relative quiet inside. Leaning against the sink, I stare at my reflection in the mirror. My cheeks are flushed, my eyes wide and bright. I look... alive. Vibrant. She's nothing like the dull, life-less woman I've seen staring back at me for months.

"Get it together, Jennifer," I mutter, splashing cold water on my face. "He's just a guy. Probably another Felix waiting to happen."

I take a deep breath, smoothing down my dress and running a hand through my hair. It's just attraction, I tell myself. A fleeting moment of connection in a sea of strangers. Nothing more.

I straighten my spine, shoulders squared as I push open the bathroom door. The music hits like a wall, an onslaught of sound and flashing lights. I brace myself, matching my internal mantra to the beat: *Don't look. Don't hope. Don't fall.*

Love is a trap, I remind myself. *A beautiful lie wrapped in shiny paper and tied with a bow of false promises.* I've been down that road before, and I've got the emotional scars to prove it. No matter how intense his gaze is, no matter how that smile makes my insides liquify, I'm not falling for it again.

The dance floor comes into view, and I spot Anna and Peter, locked in an intimate embrace. They're swaying to a rhythm all their own, lost in each other's eyes. The familiar pang of longing tugs at my chest, but I force it down. I'm happy for them, truly. But their kind of love? It's just not in the cards for me.

Shaking off the melancholy threatening to settle over me, I make my way to the bar. I need another drink, something to match this bitter taste in my mouth.

"Whiskey, neat," I tell the bartender as I slide onto a stool. It's not my usual choice, but tonight calls for something with a bite.

As I wait for my drink, I can't help but let my eyes wander. I'm not looking for him, I tell myself. I'm just... observing. Yeah, that's it. But the disappointment that settles in my stomach when I don't see those broad shoulders or that mess of black hair tells a different story.

The bartender sets my drink in front of me, and I wrap my fingers around the cool glass. I take a sip, relishing the burn as it slides down my throat. It's grounding, reminding me why I'm here. Yes, I'm here to have fun, but I'm not here to lose myself. Not again.

I'm about to take another sip when I pause. A prickle of

awareness crawls over my skin. Slowly, I lower my glass and look up. There he is.

He's on the other side of the bar; his gaze locks on me with an intensity that steals my breath. A small smile plays at the corners of his lips, knowing and mysterious all at once. My heart stutters in my chest, and I feel a flush creeping up my neck.

Look away, screams a voice in my head. But I don't. Maybe it's the alcohol kicking in, or maybe I'm just tired of playing it safe. Whatever it is, I hold his gaze, chin lifting in a silent challenge.

His smile widens as he raises his glass in a mock toast. The move is so smooth, so effortlessly charming, that I nearly laugh. Instead, I mimic the gesture, lifting my glass with a wry smirk.

What am I doing? This isn't me. I don't flirt with strangers across crowded bars. I don't engage in these wordless exchanges that crackle with tension and possibility. And yet... I can't seem to look away. His eyes hold mine, a silent conversation unfolding between us. He quirks an eyebrow, posing a playful challenge. I feel my lips twitch in response, fighting a smile.

He leans forward, elbows on the bar, the stretch of his shirt across his chest drawing my gaze. My throat tightens; I swallow hard.

No, Jennifer. This is dangerous territory.

But I can't help myself. I tilt my head, considering him. What would his name be? Something strong and masculine. Jacob, maybe? Or James? It suits him—this air of quiet confidence, the way he commands attention without saying a word.

He mirrors my tilt, amusement gleaming in his eyes. I feel a laugh bubble up, unexpected and real. This is ridiculous.

We’re playing a silent game across a crowded bar, and I’m enjoying it more than I should.

He picks up a cocktail napkin, scribbling something on it. My heart races as he holds it up. But instead of a name or number, it's a simple sketch. A crown. I furrow my brow, confused.

He grins, pointing at me, then looks back at the drawing. And suddenly, I get it. A princess. He's calling me a princess.

I roll my eyes dramatically, but I can feel the blush creeping up my neck. I grab my own napkin, quickly sketching a stick figure with exaggerated muscles. I hold it up, pointing at him with a smirk.

His shoulders shake with silent laughter, and I feel a thrill of victory. This is fun. Harmless. It's just a bit of playful banter without the messy complications of actual conversation.

Stop it, Jenn. You know where this leads.

But I can't seem to make myself walk away. There's something intoxicating about this wordless exchange, the way we're connecting without having to navigate the minefield of small talk and first impressions.

He raises his glass again, this time with a question in his eyes. An invitation. My heart pounds.

This is it. It's time for me to make a decision.

Chapter 2

Jennifer

I grip my glass, my mind a whirlwind of conflicting thoughts. It's just a drink; it doesn't have to mean anything. But I'm all too familiar with how easily I can let myself fall into the trap of wishful thinking, and how much it hurts when reality inevitably crashes in. I take a deep breath, trying to steady myself. I can't give in to this temptation. I won't.

With a regretful smile, I shake my head and raise my glass one final time in a silent salute before turning away and let the last bit of whiskey burn its way down my throat.

As much as my heart yearns for me to accept his drink invitation, I resist and stand up from my seat. I maneuver through the crowd, feeling the rhythm of the music pulsing through my body. The dance floor is alive with people moving in sync, some lost in romantic embraces while others laugh and twirl without a care in the world. I spot Anna and Peter intertwined, completely enraptured by each other.

The music shifts, adopting a seductive beat that sweeps everyone into a collective sway. I find myself drawn in, closing my eyes and surrendering to the moment. For a fleeting second, I let myself believe this could be enough.

But then I feel it—that familiar tingling sensation on my skin that signifies he's watching me. My heart races and my senses go into overdrive, but I resist the urge to search for him in the crowd. A flush spreads across my cheeks and neck, and I have to fight back the trembling in my hands. I should walk away and find Anna, end the night here.

Yet, instead of leaving, I let myself give into his unseen gaze. My movements become more sensual and fluid, running my hands through my hair and arching my back slightly. It's not like me to put on a show for strangers at a bar.

But something about this feels exhilarating—knowing he's watching me and responding to every inch of my body. Our silent dance is intoxicating, and I can't help but move with more purpose. My fingers trail down my neck in a way that would normally make me blush, but now only adds fuel to this fire between us.

I slowly open my eyes, drawn to him like a magnet. He's leaning against the bar, his striking green eyes fixed on me. A smile spreads across his face, and I feel it like a physical touch.

This is reckless. I know I shouldn't play this game, but right now, I feel alive. Desired. In control. The logical part of my brain screams for caution, reminding me why I swore off men like him. But my body has other plans. Slowly, I turn, giving him a glimpse of my back, glancing over my shoulder to meet his gaze once more.

He pushes off the bar, taking a step toward me. My heart skips, caught between excitement and fear. What am I doing? What do I even want?

Before I can make a decision, the song changes. The spell

is broken, and I'm left standing alone on the dance floor, breathless and unsure. I need some fresh air. And some time to think things through.

I pivot to leave and collide with a solid chest. My breath catches as I look up into the face that has captivated me all night, now just inches away, his eyes blazing with something that makes my skin tingle.

His warm breath brushes against my face invitingly. "Well hello there, Princess. What a coincidence running into you like this."

My heart skips a beat at the sound of his voice—deep, smooth with a hint of playfulness. Normally I would be bristling at being called Princess," but instead, I lean into it and him.

"Hello yourself, Prince Charming," I retort, surprising even myself. "Here to sweep me off my feet?"

A smile spreads across his face as his eyes crinkle at the corners. "Only if you want to be swept off your feet."

A new song, with a lively beat floats through the air, and without a word being exchanged, we begin to move in perfect harmony. His large hands confidently find their place on my hips, while mine settle onto his broad shoulders. It's as if our bodies know a dance that our minds haven't quite learned yet.

We sway together, the electric heat between us intensifying. I'm taken aback by how easily we fall into sync and how deeply our exchange affects me. His touch is strong yet gentle, guiding without being controlling.

"So, Princess," he murmurs, his lips brushing against my ear. "What's your story?"

I burst out laughing, tilting my head back in amusement. "Wouldn't you love to know?"

"I actually would," he admits, his eyes sparkling with

curiosity. "Let me guess... corporate lawyer by day, undercover superhero by night?"

I snort, unable to contain my amusement. "Close. Replace 'superhero' with 'binge-watcher of Netflix' and you've got it."

He chuckles, the deep sound reverberating through his chest. "A woman after my own heart. What's your favorite show?"

"It depends." I raise an eyebrow. "Are you going to judge me based on my answer?"

"Always," he teases. "but I'll be fair."

I roll my eyes, but I can't help the smile tugging at my lips. "Fine. It's a toss-up between 'The Great British Bake Off' and 'True Crime Documentaries'. Judge away, Your Highness."

"Interesting combination," he muses, his hand splaying across my lower back. "Sweet and deadly. I like it."

The music swells, and we move closer, our bodies fitting together like puzzle pieces. I should feel uncomfortable with this level of intimacy with a stranger, but instead, I feel... safe. Seen.

"And you, Prince Charming?" I ask. "What's your poison?"

He grins wickedly. "Oh, I'm more of a 'Bridgerton' man myself. I live for the drama and the corsets."

I laugh, feeling light and carefree for the first time in ages. "I knew there was something regal about you."

His laughter fills me, warm and inviting. It's been so long since I've felt this playful and carefree. It's almost intoxicating, and I find myself wanting more.

"Alright, Your Highness," I say, quirking an eyebrow. "If we're playing twenty questions, it's my turn. What's your day job when you're not ruling your kingdom?"

He grins, spinning me out and pulling me back in with

effortless grace. "I'm a professional cat herder. It's a niche market, but someone's got to do it."

I snort, unable to contain my amusement. "Oh really? And how does one get into such a prestigious field?"

"Years of rigorous training," he replies solemnly. "You have to master the art of looking aloof while secretly craving attention. Cats respect that."

Our banter continues, each question more ridiculous than the last.

As our laughter subsides, he leans in close, his breath tickling my ear. "What do you say we continue this riveting conversation over another drink, Princess?"

For a moment, I hesitate, feeling the same doubts I had before creeping back into my mind. But then he smiles at me, with that mischievous twinkle in his eye, and I find myself nodding without thinking.

My skin feels like it's humming with anticipation as he leads me through the packed bar with a light touch on my back. I can sense him behind me, his body heat radiating towards mine through the small space between us.

Finally, we reach a quiet corner of the bar and he gestures for me to sit down. As I perch on the bar stool, I can't help but notice how close we are. Our knees almost touch and I feel tiny sparks of excitement running up my spine.

"What will you have, Princess?" he asks.

I turn to the bartender. "I'll have a Jack Daniels on the rocks, please."

When I turn back, he's grinning, eyes alight with surprise and admiration. "Impressive choice," he says, ordering the same for himself.

As our drinks arrive, he raises his glass in a silent toast. I quickly follow suit. Our eyes lock over the rim of our glasses, and suddenly, words feel unnecessary.

His gaze is penetrating, searching. I feel exposed and vulnerable, but not uncomfortably. My breath catches as his intense stare flickers down to my lips before returning to mine.

The air around us crackles with unspoken potential. I know I should break this dangerous tension by looking away. But I can't. His magnetic presence has me spellbound and drawn in.

I let the rich whiskey slide down my throat, warming me from the inside out. As I savor the smoky flavor, the opening chords of a familiar song drift through the air. My stomach clenches as the melody takes me back to a time I'd rather forget.

I can't help but roll my eyes. “Oh, great. Just what we need—another sappy love song.”

Mister handsome raises an eyebrow, his lips quirking into an amused smile. “Not a fan of romantic ballads?"

“Please,” I scoff, setting my glass down with a little more force than necessary. “It's all just saccharine nonsense designed to manipulate emotions.”

He leans in, his green eyes dancing with curiosity. “And what's wrong with a little emotion? Isn't that what love's all about?”

I snort, unable to keep the bitterness from my voice. "Love? Please. It's just a marketing ploy created by greeting card companies to sell more chocolate.”

His eyebrows shoot up and I prepare for him to backtrack or disagree. But instead, he laughs—a genuine sound that sends shivers down my spine.

“Greeting card companies? And here I thought it was a conspiracy by jewelers and florists.”

His reaction and the whiskey warming my veins embolden me to lean in closer. “Oh no, they're all in on it too.

The whole thing's a scam. Happily ever after? More like 'putting up with each other until death do us part.'"

He nods sagely, a mock-serious expression on his face. "Ah yes, the sacred vows. 'I promise to love you, even when you leave dirty dishes in the sink and hog all the blankets.'"

A surprised laugh bubbles up from my chest. "And let's not forget, 'I'll stand by you, as long as you don't expect me to remember your mother's birthday or pick up my socks.'"

He grins, raising his glass in a toast. "To love: a beautiful delusion that keeps therapists in business."

I clink my glass against his, marveling at the easy banter between us. Most guys would have run for the hills by now, muttering about 'crazy chicks' and 'commitment issues.' But he's not only keeping up; he's matching me quip for quip.

"I'm impressed," I admit, the words slipping out before I can stop them. "Most men would be halfway to the door by now, hearing my thoughts on love and relationships."

His eyes soften, a hint of vulnerability peeking through his playful facade. "Maybe I'm not most men," he says quietly, his gaze holding mine. "And I enjoy a challenge."

I quirk an eyebrow, intrigued. "Is that so? And what, pray tell, makes you think I'm a challenge worth accepting?"

His gaze grows heated and intense. "Call it intuition," he murmurs, "or perhaps just... a hunch." His fingers trail along the back of my hand, sending tingles up my arm. "There's a fire in you, Princess, that I find... captivating."

I swallow hard, my heart pounding. "And what if I told you," I whisper, "that this fire you find so captivating has been extinguished? Burned out by one too many disappointments?"

His expression shifts, a flicker of understanding passing across his features. "Then I'd say," he whispers back, "that it's my mission to stoke those embers until the flames burn brighter than ever before."

The air between us crackles with unspoken promise; the tension is palpable. I find myself leaning closer, drawn in by the intensity of his gaze and the sincerity in his words.

"And what if," I murmur, "I told you that I'm afraid of getting burned again?"

His thumb brushes across the back of my hand, a gentle caress. "Then I'd say, Princess, that I'm more than willing to take that risk. To prove to you that not every flame will leave you in ashes."

I hold his gaze, searching for any sign of deception, any hint that he's merely playing a game. But all I see is a raw, honest yearning that resonates deep within me.

I take another sip of my drink, larger this time. "Let's play a game to get to know each other better," I suggest, eager to change the subject. "Truth or dare."

He raises an eyebrow at me with a smirk. "Alright. I'm in, if you are. Truth."

Pretending to think for a moment, I tap my chin. "What's your most embarrassing moment?"

The prince laughs, running a hand through his hair. "Easy. Junior prom. I tried to impress my date with a backflip. Ended up flat on my face in front of the entire school."

I can't help but giggle at the mental image. "Smooth moves, Your Highness."

"Your turn," he says, leaning forward. "Truth or dare?"

"Truth."

His eyes gleam. "First kiss. Spill."

I groan, feeling heat creep up my neck. "Tommy Wilson, eighth grade. Behind the bleachers. It was... wet."

He laughs, and I find myself leaning closer, drawn in by his warmth.

"Truth or dare?" I ask, my voice lower than I intended.

"Dare," he says, his eyes never leaving mine.

My heart races. I should keep it light, fun. Instead, I hear myself say, "I dare you to tell me your best pickup line."

His grin turns wicked. Then he leans in close, his breath hot against my ear. "If I had a star for every time you brightened my day, I'd be holding a galaxy in my hand."

I burst out laughing, equal parts amused and charmed. "That was terrible!"

"Terribly effective," he counters with a wink. "Your turn. Truth or dare?"

I hesitate, caught between caution and curiosity. "Truth," I say finally.

His eyes darken, his voice dropping to a husky whisper. "What's the first thing you noticed about me?"

I gulp, suddenly aware of our closeness. His scent surrounds me — a mix of cologne and something uniquely his. I should lie, guard my emotions. But under the influence of alcohol and his proximity, I feel reckless.

"Your eyes," I confess, barely above a whisper. "They're... intense."

His gaze drops to my lips, and for a moment, I think he might kiss me. My body hums with anticipation, every nerve ending on high alert. I should feel uncomfortable and exposed, but instead, I feel a thrill of power. I'm playing with fire, and for the first time in forever, I don't want to stop.

"Truth or dare?" I ask, trying to steady my voice.

His eyes meet mine, a challenge sparking in their depths. "Dare."

I lean back, considering him. I could keep it safe and dare him to do something silly. But that's not where this is heading. I take a deep breath, steeling myself. "I dare you to tell me something you like in a partner. Something... intimate."

He leans in closer, his voice low and sensual. “I like someone who knows what they want and isn't afraid to ask for it.”

I swallow hard, warmth pooling in my belly. I've never been that bold. But tonight, I want to be.

He gazes at me, never breaking eye contact. “Truth or dare?”

I ponder for a moment before whispering, “Truth.”

His lips curl into a slow, mischievous grin. “What's one thing you can't stand in a partner? What's a deal-breaker for you?”

I chew on my bottom lip, considering his question. “I can't tolerate passivity. I need someone who meets me half-way, who puts in equal effort. I won't be the only one trying or putting myself out there.”

He nods in understanding. “That makes sense. For me, it's games; I want someone who's open and honest with their communication.”

The air between us shifts, the tension ratcheting up a notch. I take a sip of my drink, the smoky flavor grounding me.

“Truth or dare?”

His eyes gleam wickedly. "Dare."

Leaning closer, I softly challenge him, “I dare you to tell me a secret. Something you've never told anyone else.”

He hesitates, searching my eyes before leaning in close enough for his breath to tickle my ear. "I enjoy roughness in bed. The push and pull, give and take. A partner who's not afraid to leave marks or be marked." My pulse quickens at his words; instead of being shocked or disgusted, I'm intrigued and aroused.

“Your turn, Princess,” he murmurs, his lips brushing my ear. “Truth or dare?”

I close my eyes, gathering my courage. Then I look at him, my voice steady. “Truth.”

His eyes darken and his voice lowers into a deep growl. "What's your deepest, darkest fantasy? The one that keeps you up at night, sweating and yearning? The one you're afraid to confess because of judgment?"

My heart races as I hesitate; I could lie but I don't want to. I want him to know the truth; I want to see his reaction. "I... I fantasize about complete surrender, being taken utterly and completely. Giving up control and letting someone else take the reins."

His eyes widen in surprise and heat as he leans closer, his voice husky with desire. “That's fucking hot.”

His words embolden me. I lean back, eyes fixed on his. “What's your favorite part of a woman's body? The one that drives you wild, that you can't resist?”

His gaze drops to my lips, then lowers, lingering on the swell of my breasts and the curve of my hips. “The small of her back,” he murmurs. “That delicate arch, that sensitive spot right above her ass. I love how it feels under my hands and how she responds when I touch her there.”

I swallow hard, my pulse racing. His words have ignited a fire within me, one I'm not sure I can—or want to—extinguish. His eyes lock onto mine, a mischievous glint sparkling in their depths.

“There's another spot,” he whispers, his voice husky. “More... taboo.”

I lean in, curiosity overriding my usual reservations. “Tell me.”

His lips brush my ear. “The rim of her asshole. So sensitive, so taboo. The way she gasps when you touch her there.”

To my surprise, I don't recoil. Instead, a thrum of curiosity pulses through me. Am I losing my mind, or simply captivated by his raw honesty?

"Your turn," he says with a deep desire in his eyes. "Same question. What's your favorite spot?"

I bite my lip, considering. "The nape of the neck," I confess. "That place where the hairline meets skin. I love running my fingers through it, and gripping it when things get... intense."

The words spill out before I can stop them, surprising even myself. I've never been this open, this vulnerable, with someone I barely know. But there's something about him, about the way he sees me, that makes me want to drop my carefully constructed walls.

A slow grin spreads across his face. "Damn, Princess. You're full of surprises."

We trade questions, each sip of our drinks lowering our inhibitions. I learn about his fascination with bondage; I reveal my desire to be dominated. Each revelation thickens the tension between us, charged with a raw energy that makes my skin tingle. Part of me should feel disgusted, but instead, I lean in, eager for more.

"Last question," he says as he leans closer to me. "What's your deepest forbidden desire?"

I hesitate for a moment; a part of me wants to shut down and end this madness before it consumes me. But another part urges me forward, daring me to take a risk.

Something about him and this night has awakened a side of me that I've kept hidden for so long. A part of me that craves the unknown and thrives on the thrill of the forbidden. And in this moment, I find myself wanting to embrace that side of me, no matter the consequences.

"Having sex with a stranger," I whisper, "in a public place

where we might get caught. And being unapologetically loud when he fucks me."

Admitting it feels like a plunge into icy water—exhilarating and terrifying. But the hunger in his eyes sends a rush of heat through me. His hand slides onto my thigh, and I feel the warmth radiating from his palm.

I want to move closer, to feel his body against mine, but I resist the urge. His hand trails further up my inner thigh, sending shivers through my body. I gasp as he tightens his grip and turns his palm upward, silently inviting me to join him.

My mind races as the intensity of our unspoken desires fill the air. My hands start to sweat as I struggle between reason and desire.

The temptation is overwhelming, like a siren's call tempting me into dangerous waters. I know I should resist, for fear of getting hurt. But at this moment, I'm consumed by an intense desire to throw caution to the wind.

For once, I long to silence the voice of reason and leave behind the ghosts of my past. I want nothing more than to revel in the unknown and embrace the intoxicating tension between us.

My hand hovers over his, trembling slightly as I contemplate my next move. The rational part of me still urges me to pull back and retreat. But the wild, untamed part of me that has been awakened tonight refuses to be ignored.

I meet his gaze. In his eyes, I see desire—and a question.

This is it. The moment of truth. Do I leap or retreat?

Chapter 3

Jennifer

Without hesitation, I slip my hand into his. A jolt of electricity courses through me. He pays the bill quickly, his grip on my hand firm as he leads me through the crowded club.

As we make our way through the pulsing dance floor, doubts start to creep in. This isn't like me at all—I'm usually cautious and would never follow a stranger, no matter how alluring they may seem. Yet here I am, letting this mysterious man lead me away from the safety of the crowd.

I should find Anna, have her talk some sense into me. But his touch drowns out reason, a thrilling pull I can't resist.

He maneuvers effortlessly through the throng, pulling me along. The pounding music fades as we step into a dimly lit hallway. My heart pounds. Is he taking me to the restroom? A surge of excitement mixes with fear—I've never been one for public displays of affection.

Instead of heading to the bathroom, he leads me down a dimly lit hallway. The sound of music and chatter from the party fades into the background as we reach a door labeled

"Do Not Enter." Without hesitation, he pushes it open and pulls me inside.

The stairwell is dim and industrial, with rough concrete walls and metal railings. The club's throbbing bass fades behind us, replaced by the mingling scent of his cologne and the building's musty odor.

As we climb, the sharp echo of our footsteps matches my racing heartbeat. His thumb traces slow circles on my skin, a gentle gesture that both calms my nerves and stokes a growing fire within me.

Fear should be flooding my senses, but it's not. It's excitement. And him.

We pause on a wide platform and he turns to face me, his intense gaze holding mine as he speaks in a deep and authoritative tone.

"Princess, tell me... do you want me to be your Prince? The one who fulfills all those naughty fantasies you've been hiding?"

My breath catches in my throat at his question. Yes, more than anything. But admitting it feels like breaking down my last defenses. He inches closer, his lips brushing against my ear as he continues.

"If you say yes, I will make your naughty dreams come true." A small moan escapes me as I imagine his hands on me, his mouth exploring every inch of my body. The overwhelming need that washes over me is exhilarating, and I answer.

"Yes."

His grin widens, promising all sorts of wicked delights. He moves closer, pressing me against the concrete wall with his body. His hand slides up my side and over my waist, resting on my breast. I lean into him, gasping softly as he circles my nipple with his thumb.

"Anyone could walk in here, just like we did," I say as I look down the metal staircase, my heart pounding in my chest. The faint sounds of the party echo up the stairs, a reminder of the world we've left behind.

A slow smile spreads across his face, "Exactly." His eyes lock with mine. "And I know something that would make this experience even more thrilling."

I raise an eyebrow. "Oh really? And what might that be?"

He steps back, producing a red silk tie from his pocket.

"Well well, look at Prince Charming carrying around bondage gear now. Your love for control is real."

"That it is." He runs the tie along my bare arm. "I want to bind your wrists together and secure them above your head to the metal stairs. I want you completely at my mercy while I pleasure you."

A wave of heat washes over me as I imagine myself bound and helpless. I nibble on my bottom lip, a habit I can't seem to break when I'm nervous or turned on.

He notices and leans in. "What do you say, Princess? Shall we satisfy both our cravings?"

"Yes, please," I whisper.

Without wasting a second, he takes my wrists in his hand and begins to bind them together. I can't help but feel a thrill of anticipation. I'm playing with fire, and I love every second of it.

"Raise your arms."

I comply, the cool metal railing pressing into my skin as he ties my hands above my head. The sound of fabric rustling against the metal, heightens the thrill of this forbidden encounter. His gaze roams over me, intense and hungry. There's no turning back.

"Look at you, Princess," he murmurs against my neck as one hand trails down it. "So beautiful and craving my touch."

He cups one breast, and I'm glad I'm not wearing a bra when he teases my sensitive skin through the fabric.

“Now listen carefully,” he says, lifting my chin to meet his intense gaze. “When I ask you a question, I want a clear 'yes' or 'no' answer. Understood?”

“Yes.” I gasp when he pinches my nipple.

“Perfect.”

His fingers slip beneath the fabric of my dress, tracing along the sensitive skin of my inner thigh and making their way towards my throbbing core. “Do you want me to touch you there? To feel how wet and eager you are for me.”

“Yes, please.”

“A needy little thing,” he chuckles, his voice dripping with dark promises. “Well, since you asked so politely…”

In one fluid motion, his skilled fingers glide back and forth over the delicate lace of my thong, igniting a blazing inferno within me. My body coils with anticipation and I arch my back in pleasure, a throaty moan escaping my lips.

“Yes, that's it. Let everyone hear the sound of your desire.”

The flush of heat radiating from my skin intensifies as I writhe under his touch.

“Please,” I beg.

He withdraws his hand, eliciting a desperate whimper from me. But before I can protest, he's pressing his body against mine and crushing his lips onto mine.

The world narrows to the taste of him and I lose myself in the kiss. When he pulls away, we're both panting.

“I want you to look at me,” he demands. “I want to see the hunger in your eyes as I touch you.”

His hands grip the hem of my dress, slowly inching it up my thighs until it's bunched around my waist. My heart races as he hooks his fingers into the waistband of my panties and tugs them down agonizingly slowly.

His warm breath tickles the skin of my legs, “You're such a good girl, staying still for me.” He tucks the discarded lace into his jacket pocket before standing.

My breathing quickens as he leans in close, his hot breath tickling my ear. “How do you want me to pleasure you?”

My thoughts are a jumbled mess as I try to form a coherent response. “Ravish me,” I finally manage to say.

A wicked grin spreads across his face as he meets my gaze. “As you wish, my Princess.” And with that, he descends upon me, pushes my legs apart, and buries his face between my thighs. Pleasure courses through me and I moan unabashedly as his tongue explores every inch of my slick folds.

“You taste so good. I could spend all night feasting on this sweet cunt,” he murmurs against my skin, causing delicious vibrations to shoot through me.

But it's not enough. My hips buck against him in search of more stimulation. “Please,” I beg, my need becoming almost unbearable.

He slips two fingers inside me, curling and pressing against my walls as his tongue continues its relentless assault on my clit. Every stroke, every twist sends shocks of pleasure shooting through me.

But it's still not enough. I need more.

I strain against the bonds. “Please, more.”

His fingers slip out as he chuckles, then they move up to tease the tight pucker of my anus. I gasp at the foreign sensation.

“Have you ever let anyone touch you here?”

I shake my head, unable to form words as he continues his gentle caresses. “Can I show you how amazing it feels,” he whispers, his breath hot against my belly, “to have me play with your tight asshole while I pleasure your dripping wet pussy?”

Desire floods every inch of my being at the thought of him taking control and introducing me to something I've never experienced before.

“Yes, please,” I moan, unable to resist his offer.

His touch is gentle but purposeful as he teases and massage my tight asshole with my own arousal.

“Do you like how it feels?”

“I love it,” I moan, my hips bucking against him in desperate need.

He hums in satisfaction before using his hot tongue to expertly lap at my swollen clit while his finger circles my quivering hole. The contrast between his delicate touch and primal action sends waves of heat through me, driving me wild.

“Arch your beautiful body into my touch,” he commands. “Show me how much you crave me fucking you like this.”

His words are filthy and intoxicating, dripping with raw lust that only serves to inflame me further.

“Do you need more?”

“Yes! Oh god, yes!”

In one smooth motion, he pushes his broad finger into my tight and trembling ass. The sensation overwhelms me - a delicious mix of pleasure and pain that sends me spiraling towards madness.

His digit moves in and out, slow and gentle at first, then increasing the pace until my body is tense with anticipation.

“That's it, take my finger like a good girl,” he growls. “I'm going to make you come so hard, your whole body will shatter.”

His tongue joins in on the action, flicking and swirling

over my sensitive clit while his fingers continue their relentless assault. Every nerve ending in my body is on fire, and I can feel myself teetering on the edge of bliss.

"Tell me when you're going to come," he demands.

With his skilled mouth on my clit and his fingers working me into a frenzy, I reach the peak of pleasure within seconds.

"Oh god...I'm... I'm coming," I scream before everything goes white and explodes into millions of fragments behind my closed eyes. But he doesn't stop there. Instead, he keeps going, driving me further and further into ecstasy until I'm completely spent and breathless.

As I come down from my high, I look down, my gaze meeting his, and the sight of him sends a fresh surge of heat through me.

His eyes are filled with an intoxicating blend of lust and satisfaction, a wicked grin tugging at the corners of his lips that are still moist and glistening from my release.

He stands and presses his body against mine; the rough fabric of his pants is a delicious contrast to the softness of my skin.

"You came so beautifully for me, Princess." His lips brush over mine. "But this, my dear, is only the beginning."

Chapter 4

Jennifer

His words ignite a wild inferno within me, and I can't help but vocalize the desires he arouses in me.

"Fuck me. I need to feel your cock deep inside of me."

His expression changes, a hungry intensity replacing the earlier softness. Without a word, he reaches up and loosens the silk tie binding my wrists, then reties it to the railing in front of me. The new position forces me to lean forward, my hands resting on the cold metal.

"What are you doing?" I ask.

"Making you more comfortable." His hands trail down my back as he adds. "And giving me better access to every inch of you."

The cool air kisses my skin as he pushes the fabric of my dress higher up my waist, creating a trail of goosebumps in its path. The sensation of his intense gaze on me, possessive and hungry, while I stand in this vulnerable position is electrifying.

His palms, firm and possessive, run along the curves of my back.

"Do you know what you look like right now, Princess?

Tied up, bent over, your curves on full display for me. Fucking irresistible."

Heat prickles across my skin, a delicious tension coiling in my stomach. He steps closer, pressing himself against my back so that I can feel his hard length through his jeans. My grip on the railing tightens as I push back against him, desperate for more.

"I want to be inside you," he whispers while grinding his hips against mine. "To feel your tight pussy wrap around me, taking all that I have."

A throaty moan escapes my lips as I push back against him, craving more of his touch. "Please," I beg, my voice thick with need. "Fuck me."

His hot breath fans across my ear as he chuckles lowly.

"Oh, Princess," he purrs, his hand sliding down to squeeze my ass possessively. "You have no idea how much you turn me on. When you beg like that, it drives me wild."

In an instant, the charged silence is broken by the sound of his jeans unzipping. He pulls out his large, thick cock, a small bead of pre-cum glistening on the tip. With practiced ease, he tears open a condom wrapper and rolls it down his length.

Our gazes lock as he pumps himself with one hand.

"Do you want this?"

I nod, incapable of forming words.

"Good. Because I plan on giving it to you so good."

He grips my hips. "Arch your back, and spread those legs for me."

I comply, pushing my butt out and arching my spine in this vulnerable position. It's thrilling to be so exposed, to feel his primal gaze devouring every inch of my body.

"Fuck." His palm glides over my skin like a flame. "You look so damn hot like this. Open and ready for me." His fingers trace the small of my back, igniting sparks of arousal within me. “And that spot on your lower back... it's incredibly sexy.”

His words play with my mind, making me feel wanted, turned on, and desirable in a way I’ve never experienced before.

My previous sexual experiences were nice, comfortable even, but they don't compare to the raw, primal need that is consuming me now. For a moment, I question how I could have such intense chemistry with someone who is practically a stranger. But as soon as his fingers dig into my flesh and his hard cock glides against my slick folds, pleasure takes over and all rational thoughts disappear.

Waves of pleasure wash over me as he teases my entrance, coating himself in my wetness. I can feel the heat pulsing between my thighs and I push back against him, craving to feel him inside of me.

“Please,” I moan.

“That's it, Princess. Tell me how badly you want this.”

The head of his cock presses against my entrance. I spread my legs wider, arching my back further, inviting him inside. Nothing else exists in this moment—only his ragged breaths and the promise of bliss.

“Take me, hard,” I plead, the desperation spilling out.

In one powerful thrust, he enters me and I cry out in pleasure. My fingers tighten their grip on the railing as I push back into him, seeking even more delicious friction.

Suddenly, a door creaks open. Hushed voices break the intimacy, and panic seizes me. I struggle against the silk ties, trying to glimpse down the stairs. Shadows dance in the dim light before the door shuts again, leaving only our ragged breathing.

My Prince chuckles softly. “Looks like we almost got

caught, Princess," he leans in and whispers. "But maybe they're just pretending to leave. Maybe they heard you moaning and now they're listening to how I'm making you climax."

The thought of being discovered, of someone hearing the intimate sounds of our bodies melding together, only adds to the intensity of my arousal.

His hands grasp my hips with a fierce strength, his fingers digging into the flesh on my backside as he spreads my cheeks apart and starts to trace circles around my tight entrance.

"Can I play with this little hole again?"

I press myself back into him, earning an approving grunt from him.

"I love how eager you are for me, my naughty little princess."

With a slick finger coated in my own arousal, he presses it past the tight ring of muscle. I gasp at the intrusion, but the discomfort is quickly replaced by intense pleasure.

The dual sensations of being taken in both holes is almost too much for me to handle, but somehow my body craves it more than anything. "You love being filled up, don't you." he murmurs, while thrusting his dick into me with unrelenting fervor.

"Yes," I gasp, unable to deny the truth.

He chuckles darkly and presses his fingers deeper inside of my ass, hitting just the right spot that sends pleasure coursing through my veins. I grind back against him, meeting every one of his thrusts with equal fervor. My knuckles turn whiter as my climax builds within me, the pleasure coursing through my veins like a raging river.

"I'm so close."

"Then come for me," he commands with a thrust that

propels me into pure bliss. My entire body quivers and tightens around him, squeezing him in a way that causes him to find his own release.

Breathless and spent, he collapses onto me, his hot breath tickling my neck. We remain intertwined, savoring the aftermath of our intense release. As our breathing steadies, he bends to press his lips against the side of my neck, the gentle touch sending shivers through me. It starkly contrasts the passionate intensity we just shared. His warm breath and the roughness of his stubble heighten the lingering sensations.

"You were stunning. Absolutely breathtaking."

I smile, basking in the familiar warmth of his praise that never fails to ignite something within me. For once, I feel no need to hide or suppress my impulses. Instead, I revel in the afterglow, savoring every remaining sensation of his touch.

"Thank you," I whisper, barely audible. "For fulfilling my wildest dreams."

He wraps his arms tighter around me and chuckles softly against my back.

"The pleasure was all mine, darling."

Once he removes and discards the condom, I observe as he skillfully unties the silk bindings that held me captive moments ago. As reality slowly sets in after our intense encounter, a wave of vulnerability washes over me.

I flex my wrists, wincing at the tenderness, but he reacts quickly and massages the marks left by the ties with tender care.

His actions make my heart flutter with both excitement and fear. But instead of embracing these powerful emotions, I resort to my usual defense mechanism. "So, do you always treat your women like this? Because I have to say, it's quite the experience."

His gaze locks onto mine. "Women?" he repeats. "You

think I do this with just any woman, Princess?" The rumble in his voice is a warning that I'm skating on thin ice.

I open my mouth to respond, to defend myself with more sarcasm, more walls built from words. But he cuts me off, his voice a low, fervent whisper.

"I'm not a man who fucks a different woman every weekend, Princess. I'm not the cliché you're trying to paint me as."

His words catch me off guard, their sincerity disarming. I want to apologize, to explain the fear beneath my sarcastic remarks. But before I can speak, his hand cups the back of my neck with a firm yet gentle touch. Our eyes hold each other's in silence, a moment of truth. Then he presses his lips against mine in a searing kiss that leaves me breathless.

His lips move against mine with desperation and passion, as if pouring all his words and emotions into this one act. I melt into him, my body pressing against his as my hands tangle in his hair.

He pulls me even closer, deepening the kiss, while his other hand rests on the small of my back. The taste of him, the sensation of him against me, and the raw hunger in his touch is overwhelming and all-consuming. His kiss feels like he's claiming me as his own.

A flurry of thoughts and emotions race through my mind, leaving me feeling terrified, exhilarated, confused, and aroused. Amidst the chaos, a small voice warns me to be cautious. This man has the power to consume me, break down my walls, and leave me more vulnerable than I've ever been.

Despite this warning, I choose to ignore it and give in to his touch. I want him now.

Our intimate moment is interrupted by my phone ringing loudly. We pull apart, both breathless, and I fumble for my phone with shaky hands. It's a text from Anna asking where I am.

As I read the words, reality comes crashing back in. I'm in a club with a stranger, making out in a stairwell after having had mind blowing sex. And to my surprise, I don't regret a single second.

Maybe Anna was right all along. Maybe this man is my Christmas Prince.

“My friend is looking for me. We should go back,” I say, glancing up at him.

He nods, and we quickly get dressed before heading downstairs to the main area. As we walk, I stop and turn to him. I need something to ground myself, to regain control over my emotions. But as I speak, my voice trembles, betraying the turmoil inside of me.

“Um...do you have...my...” I gesture awkwardly, unable to say the word.

He laughs, mischief dancing in his eyes. “Your panties?”

He reaches into his pocket and pulls them out, teasingly dangling them in front of me. "I think I'll hold onto these for now, Princess. As a little souvenir.”

I roll my eyes, but I can't hold back the smile that creeps onto my face. “You're impossible, you know that?”

“And you love it,” he retorts, tucking the silky fabric back into his pocket with a satisfied grin.

Despite the intimacy we just shared, it's surprising how easily we've fallen into this playful banter. There's a natural chemistry between us that both fascinates and excites me. I'm drawn to his carefree side, which balances out the intense passion we just experienced.

As we approach the bathrooms, he turns towards me and suggests, “I'll go clean up quickly. Meet me at the bar and I'll treat you to a drink.”

I nod, feeling butterflies flutter in my stomach. “Sounds great. I'll find my friend and let her know I'm still here.”

He flashes me a charming smile before disappearing into the bathroom, leaving me alone to process the whirlwind of emotions inside me.

As I enter the ladies' room, I catch a glimpse of myself in the mirror. The flushed, disheveled woman staring back at me hardly resembles the cautious and guarded Jennifer I know.

I splash cool water on my face, replaying our encounter in the stairwell with vivid clarity. The raw hunger in his gaze, his possessiveness, the pure bliss of surrendering completely —everything feels surreal yet undeniably real.

A sense of wonder washes over me. How could I, someone who is always so careful and guarded have let down their walls completely in just one evening? With him, everything feels natural and right. It's as if we've known each other for lifetimes instead of mere hours.

Suddenly, I realize that I don't even know his real name. But it doesn't matter. He is my “Christmas Prince,” a title that couldn't be more fitting. The thought brings a smile to my face and a glimmer of hope within me.

Maybe, just maybe, I'm not doomed in love after all. Perhaps love doesn’t despise me; maybe I had to sift through a few frogs and toads to find this rare and captivating specimen.

As I straighten my dress and run my fingers through my tousled hair, I feel this newfound sense of confidence and inner peace taking hold of me and I smile, knowing that I've found something rare and precious tonight.

Back on the dance floor, the bass thrums through my body, but it pales compared to the electricity still coursing through my veins. I scan the crowd, searching for Anna’s familiar blonde head.

“Jennifer!” Anna's voice cuts through the noise. She rushes towards me, relief etched on her face. “Where the hell have you been? I've been looking everywhere for you!”

I can't help the smirk that tugs at my lips. “Oh, you know... just living up to your Christmas miracle expectations.”

Anna's eyes widen, her mouth falling open in a perfect 'O'. “No way. Did you... did you meet someone?”

I shrug, trying to play it cool, but the flush creeping up my neck betrays me. “Maybe.”

“Oh my God!” she squeals, bouncing on her toes. “Who is he? Where is he? I need details, Jenn!”

I glance around, searching for his tall frame, but he's nowhere to be seen. “He's... around here somewhere.”

Peter appears, drinks in hand, eyebrow raised at Anna's excitement. “What's got you all worked up?”

“Jennifer met someone!” Anna gushes, practically vibrating with joy.

Peter chuckles, handing her a drink. “Should I start planning the wedding, then?”

Anna swats his arm playfully. “Don't tease. I just want her to find love.”

As Peter and Anna exchange playful banter, I tune them out, my focus consumed by the need to find the man who has so thoroughly captivated me. I can still feel the ghost of his touch, the taste of his kiss. Every cell in my body yearns for his touch, my longing nearly overwhelming me.

Suddenly the opening notes of Anna's favorite song fill the air, and she turns to Peter with pleading eyes. "Dance with me?"

Peter rolls his eyes good-naturedly, already setting down his drink. “How can I resist?”

I laugh, waving them off. “Go on, lovebirds. I'm going to look for my Christmas Prince.”

Navigating through the throngs of people, I spot him. He stands with his back to me, and I take a moment to appreciate the width of his shoulders and how his shirt hugs his muscular build.

My feet carry me towards him, a smile forming on my lips. But as I approach, I see a gorgeous woman approaching him. She's tall with long legs and honey-blonde hair, her face contorted in annoyance as she stops in front of him.

“Jack,” she says, hands planted on her hips. “What are you doing here?”

I freeze, my heart skipping a beat. I strain to hear his response.

“Honey, let me explain...” His deep voice carries over the noise.

Honey? My mind races, struggling to make sense of what I'm hearing. No way. He wouldn't do that. Not after everything we've shared.

The woman continues talking, frustration dripping from her every word. “I've been waiting for you for hours. You said you'd be home when I arrived.”

Home? My stomach churns as everything starts to click into place. He lives with her.

“I know, I'm sorry,” he says, filled with regret. “Something came up and time slipped away from me.”

Something came up? Is that all I’m to him? Just a distraction, an inconvenience?

The blonde woman snorts, her eyes narrowing in suspicion. “Something always comes up with you, Jack. You promised you'd be there.”

Anger surges through me along with the hurt. He

promised her. He has obligations to her. And I was just a fleeting moment of pleasure, easily discarded.

"I'm really sorry," he says softly. "I'll make it up to you."

Each word is like a dagger in my heart.

"Oh, you know how you can make it up to me," I hear her add with a suggestive raise of her eyebrows.

A wave of nausea washes over me as I listen to the intimacy between them, their familiarity and ease with each other. It confirms my worst fears—he's been lying to me this whole time.

Disappointment and heartache fill me as I realize I had been foolish to believe his lies. How many times must I fall victim to my own naive optimism before I learn?

I try to keep my composure as tears threaten to spill down my cheeks. I refuse to let him see me broken. With determination, I straighten up, turn and walk away while salvaging what little pride I have left. Fool me once; shame on him. Fool me twice; shame on me. I should have known better than to trust in the charm of a handsome stranger.

Stepping out into the chilly night air, I take a deep breath and fight back tears. Everything feels different now—colder, harsher.

Love, I remind myself, i*s nothing but a fickle and cruel mistress.* No, it's worse than that—it's a venomous snake waiting to strike at the most vulnerable moment. And as I fade into the darkness, I make a silent promise: never again will I fall for the false allure of love or a fucking Christmas Prince.

Chapter 5

Jack

I stand in front of my closet, frowning at the array of clothes before me. Suits feel too formal for a dinner at Peter and Anna's, but I want to make a good impression.

My hand hovers over a crisp button-down before moving to a soft blue sweater. Casual, but not too casual. I pair it with dark jeans, the ones Honey always says make me look "less like a youth counselor and more like a guy who actually remembers how to have fun."

As I pull on the sweater, my mind drifts to Peter and Anna. It's only been a few months since Peter started at the Youth Center, but we clicked instantly. There's something about him—his easy smile, his patience with the kids—that made me think, "This is someone I want in my corner."

I remember the day he first mentioned Anna. His whole face lit up, eyes crinkling at the corners as he talked about their weekend plans. I felt a pang then, a bittersweet reminder of how I used to feel talking about Sarah.

But there is something different about Peter and Anna's relationship. A solidity, a warmth that goes beyond the honeymoon phase.

I shake off the melancholy thoughts, focusing instead on the excitement of the evening ahead. I'm curious to finally spend some real time with Anna, to see firsthand the woman who's captured Peter's heart so completely.

I adjust my collar, smoothing down the soft wool of the sweater. “Not bad, Daniels,” I mutter to my reflection, trying to project more confidence than I feel.

My phone buzzes, and I see a text from Peter: “Looking forward to seeing you tonight, man. Anna's gone all out with the decorations. Her best friend will be joining us too.”

I type a quick reply, trying to ignore the way my stomach flips at the thought of meeting someone new. It's been a month since that night at the club, but I can't shake the memory of her—the mysterious woman who vanished like smoke after our encounter in the stairwell.

I close my eyes, and suddenly I'm there again. The dim light, the soft sounds she made as I touched her. The way she looked at me—with desire and vulnerability in equal measure. And then... nothing. She never showed up at the bar, leaving me with nothing but the lingering scent of her perfume and a head full of questions.

I've tried to find her. God knows I’ve tried. But it's like she never existed—just a fleeting moment of connection in a world that seems a lot emptier without her.

The image of Sarah flashes through my mind—Sarah, standing in our bedroom, tears streaming down her face as she confessed to cheating on me. On our anniversary, no less.

“I’m sorry, Jack,” she'd sobbed. “It just happened. I never meant to hurt you.”

I clench my fist, the old anger and hurt rising like bile in my throat. I'd thought I was past this, but the memory of that night at the club, the possibility of something real, is bringing it all back.

I shake my head, trying to clear my thoughts.

As I'm giving myself a final once-over in the mirror, my phone buzzes. Honey's face pops up on the screen, her tongue sticking out in the ridiculous selfie she insists on using for her contact photo.

I swipe to answer. “What's up, troublemaker?”

“Just checking to make sure you haven't chickened out on this dinner party,” Honey's voice chirps through the speaker. “You know, your natural habitat is dark clubs and brooding silences.”

I roll my eyes, even though she can't see me. “I'm wounded. I'll have you know I'm perfectly capable of adult socialization.”

“Uh-huh,” she says, skepticism dripping from her voice. “What are you wearing?”

“Blue sweater, dark jeans.”

There's a pause. "The soft blue sweater that makes you look like a sexy librarian, or the electric blue one that makes you look like a lost boy band member?”

I glance down at myself. “Uh, the soft blue one?"

“Thank God,” Honey sighs dramatically. “There's hope for you yet, big brother.”

“Your faith in me is overwhelming,” I deadpan.

“Someone's gotta look out for you,” she quips back. “Now, remember—smile, make eye contact, and for the love of all that is holy, do not start talking about your whiskey collection.”

“That was one time!”

“One time too many," she retorts. “Oh, and Jack?”

“Yeah?”

Her voice softens a bit. “Have fun, okay? You deserve it.”

I feel a smile tugging at my lips. “Thanks, Honey.”

“Anytime. Now go get 'em, tiger!”

I hang up, shaking my head but still smiling. Say what you will about Honey, but she always knows how to lift my spirits. Even if it's at my expense.

I think about the kids at the youth center, especially Tommy. The angry, hurting boy who reminded me so much of myself at that age. I remember the day he finally opened up, tears in his eyes as he talked about his dad leaving.

“It gets better, kid,” I’d told him, meaning every word. “It hurts like hell now, but you'll get through this. And you'll be stronger for it.”

It's time I took my own advice.

I give my apartment a final once-over before leaving. The open-plan space is a testament to my bachelor lifestyle—sleek and modern, with touches of industrial chic. Exposed brick walls contrast with the polished concrete floors, while floor-to-ceiling windows offer a stunning view of the city skyline. My prized whiskey collection gleams from the custom-built shelving unit, a reminder of Honey's earlier teasing.

As I lock up and head down the hallway, my footsteps echo in the quiet of the upscale building. The elevator doors slide open silently, and I step in, catching a glimpse of my reflection in the mirrored walls. I take a deep breath, straightening my shoulders.

When I step out into the cool evening air, I’m greeted by the bustling energy of the city. The streets are alive with the Friday night crowd—couples walking hand in hand in the snow, groups of friends laughing as they head to bars and restaurants. I make my way to my car, parked in its designated spot. As I slide into the driver's seat, I can't help but feel a mix of anticipation and nervousness about the evening ahead.

But I can't help but wonder. What if, by some miracle, I saw her again? What would I say? What would I do?

I shake off the thought. It's just a fantasy. Tonight is about reality—friends, good food.

Chapter 6

Jennifer

As I trudge through the snow-dusted streets of the city, the world around me stands in stark contrast to the turmoil raging within. The air is crisp and biting, my breath forming puffs of white in the frosty December air. The city is decked out in its Christmas best—twinkling lights adorn the storefronts, garlands and wreaths hang from the lampposts, and the distant sound of carolers fills the evening.

Yet, instead of filling me with the season's cheer, the festive displays only serve to deepen my scowl. Everywhere I look, there's another reminder of the magic I've been so cruelly denied. Magic. Right. More like a cruel joke.

I turn the corner, narrowly avoiding a cluster of carolers. Their joyful voices grate on my nerves, each note a stark contrast to the storm brewing inside me. My mind drifts, unbidden, to him. The Christmas Prince. I scoff at the ridiculous nickname, anger bubbling up inside me.

"Let it go," I mutter, shoving my hands deeper into my pockets. But my traitorous mind refuses to obey. Instead, it conjures up images of piercing green eyes, strong hands, and that infuriatingly perfect jawline. I grit my teeth, frustration mounting as I feel the familiar warmth spreading through my body.

A month. It's been a whole damn month, and still, I can't shake him. My dreams replay that night torturously—the heated glances across the bar, the electric tension during our game of truth or dare, the scorching kisses in the stairwell. Each memory is a dagger, twisting deeper with the knowledge that it was all a lie.

I pause at a crosswalk, my reflection staring back at me from a festively decorated shop window.

"You're pathetic," I tell my mirrored self. "He has someone. Someone he calls Honey, for Christ's sake." The light changes, and I storm across the street, my anger propelling me forward.

How could I have been so blind? So foolish? The intensity in his eyes, the raw passion in his touch—it had felt so real. But clearly, I'm an idiot who can't tell the difference between genuine connection and a player's game.

A couple passes by, hand in hand, lost in their own little world. I glare at their retreating backs, envy and bitterness churning in my gut.

"Why?" I whisper to the uncaring universe. "Why does this keep happening to me?"

But the universe, as always, remains stubbornly silent. The only response is the distant sound of sleigh bells and the muffled laughter from a nearby pub. I shake my head, quickening my pace.

Anna and Peter's apartment isn't far now, and I'm already regretting agreeing to this Christmas Eve gathering.

As I round the final corner, a gust of wind whips past, carrying with it the scent of cinnamon and pine. For a moment, just a fraction of a second, it reminds me of him. Of the intoxicating mix of his cologne and how erotic it felt when he tied me to the railing in that stairwell.

"Damn it." Angry tears are pricking at my eyes. I blink them away furiously, refusing to let him affect me any more than he already has. But even as I turn the corner into Anna's street, I can't help but wonder: *Will I ever learn? Or am I doomed to keep falling for the promise of love, only to have my heart shattered again and again?*

I pause at the foot of Anna and Peter's brownstone, my breath catching in my throat. The sight before me is so utterly ridiculous, that for a moment I forget why I was even upset.

"Holy reindeer," I whisper, awestruck.

Their house looks like Santa's workshop exploded. Twinkling lights drape every inch of the facade, blinking in mesmerizing patterns. An inflatable snowman towers over me, its plastic face frozen in an eternal grin. Tinsel garlands snake around the porch railings, and a giant wreath adorns the front door, complete with a red bow the size of my head.

A laugh bubbles up inside me, unbidden. Of course Anna went overboard. Why am I even surprised? My best friend's enthusiasm for Christmas makes elves look like amateurs.

I shake my head, a genuine smile tugging at my lips. It's so perfectly, ridiculously Anna that I can't help but feel a spark of warmth in my chest. This is what happens when Anna loves something—she dives in headfirst, no holds barred. And Christmas? Well, that ranks right up there with Peter on her list of loves.

Taking a deep breath, I climb the steps and ring the doorbell. Instead of a chime, I hear "Jingle Bells" played on what sounds like a kazoo.

The door flies open, and there's Anna, a vision in red and green. She's wearing a sweater that lights up, antlers on her head, and—are those jingle bell earrings?

"Jenn!" she squeals, pulling me into a bone-crushing hug. "You made it!"

Before I can respond, she yanks me inside, and I stumble across the threshold only to have my jaw drop. If I thought the outside was over-the-top, it's nothing compared to this.

Every surface gleams with tinsel and ornaments. A massive tree dominates the living room, so laden with decorations I can barely see the green. Garlands drape from the ceiling, and the air is thick with the scent of cinnamon and gingerbread.

"Wow," I manage, spinning slowly. "Anna, this is... I'm speechless."

She beams, practically vibrating with excitement. "Isn't it amazing? We really went all out this year!"

I can't help but chuckle. "I can see that. The only thing missing is real reindeer in the living room."

"Don't give her ideas," comes a warm, amused voice. Peter emerges from the kitchen, wearing a 'Santa's Favorite Ho Ho Ho' apron. He gives me a friendly nod. "Hey, Jenn. Glad you could make it."

As I take in the scene—Anna in her Christmas glory, Peter's resigned but affectionate smile, the sheer explosion of holiday cheer surrounding me—I feel something shift inside me.

"So, what culinary masterpiece have you whipped up for tonight?" I ask, quirking an eyebrow. "Let me guess, reindeer steaks with a side of elf-made mashed potatoes?"

Anna giggles, her antlers jingling. "Close! We've got honey-glazed ham, cranberry stuffing, and—drumroll, please —my famous eggnog cheesecake!"

"Sounds delicious," I say, genuinely meaning it. "Is David joining us this year?"

Peter shakes his head. “Nah, he couldn't make it. Family thing.”

I shrug, feeling surprisingly okay with the idea of a cozy threesome. That is until I catch him glancing at Anna. The look passing between them sets off alarm bells in my head and my stomach tightens.

“It is just us three tonight, right?” I ask, my voice sharper than intended.

Anna doesn't answer. Instead, she practically skips to a side table, grabbing a tall, frosted glass. “Oh! You have to try my special Christmas cocktail. It's got cranberry vodka, ginger ale, and-”

“Anna.” I cut her off, fixing her with a stare. “What aren't you telling me?”

She fidgets, jingling bell earrings, tinkling nervously. “Well... you see... I may have... invited someone else.”

I groan, pieces clicking into place. “Please tell me you didn't go into matchmaker mode again. You promised—”

“But Jenn!” Anna interrupts, eyes wide and pleading. “This guy is perfect for you! He's tall, handsome, and successful.”

“And probably has a secret family in Peru,” I finish dryly. “Anna, sweetie, I love you, but your track record with setups is... well, let's just say it's not great.”

She pouts, looking so much like a kicked puppy that I almost feel bad. Almost.

“But this time it's different!” she says. “I have a really good feeling about this one.”

I pinch the bridge of my nose, feeling a headache coming on. “Anna, honey, your 'good feelings' once led to me dating a guy who thought the earth was flat.”

Peter snorts, trying unsuccessfully to turn it into a cough when Anna glares at him.

Then she turns back to me, her eyes pleading. “Please, I promise, if this isn't the right man, I'll stop my matchmaking.”

“Fine,” I sigh, knowing resistance is futile. “But if this guy turns out to be a closet furry or believes in lizard people, I'm holding you personally responsible.”

Anna beams, relief flooding her face. “You won't regret this, I promise!”

Her eyes light up, her antlers bobbing as she leans in conspiratorially. “He's actually from Peter's new work and he's absolutely amazing.”

Peter nods, a small smile playing on his lips. “Yeah, he's pretty cool. Down-to-earth guy, you'd like him.”

I can't help but roll my eyes. “Right. I'm sure he's just perfect. Probably rescues kittens and cures cancer in his spare time, too.”

Before Anna can protest, I grab the cocktail from her hand and take a healthy sip. The sweet, spicy liquid burns its way down my throat, warming me from the inside out. At least there's alcohol to get me through this disaster in waiting.

A shrill beeping cuts through the air, making us all jump. Peter's eyes widen.

“Oh, that's the timer. Gotta check on the ham.”

As he hurries off to the kitchen, Anna turns to me, her expression softening. She reaches out and places a gentle hand on my arm.

“Jenn, sweetie, don't let what happened last month taint your belief in love. You deserve happiness.”

I snort, the bitterness rising like bile in my throat. “Oh yeah? And how would you react if the man you flirted with turned out to have a girlfriend at home? One he calls 'honey' as a pet name?”

Anna's face falls, her usual optimism dimming for a

moment. “Okay, so you have a little glitch when it comes to falling for the wrong men. But Jenn, not every guy is like that. I truly believe you'll find your match.”

“Sure,” I mutter, taking another gulp of my drink. The alcohol buzzes through my system, loosening my tongue. “The only prince I'll ever find is the one I imagine when I'm alone with my vibrator.”

Anna's eyes widen, a mix of shock and sympathy flickering across her face. “Oh, Jenn...”

But before she can launch into another pep talk, the doorbell chimes. My stomach drops as Anna's face lights up like the Christmas tree behind her.

“He's here!” she squeals.

I drain the last of my cocktail, steeling myself for whatever fresh hell Anna's matchmaking has conjured up this time.

As she rushes to the door, I can't help walking back to the table for another cocktail; I'm sure I’ll need another one tonight.

The door swings open, and I hold my breath, bracing for the reveal of Anna's latest “perfect match.” But as the newcomer steps into view, my world tilts on its axis.

There, framed in the doorway like some cruel joke of fate, stands the very man I’ve been trying to forget for the past month: The Christmas Prince himself.

Chapter 7

Jennifer

My heart lurches, then starts racing at an alarming pace against my ribs.

Anna's voice breaks through the fog in my mind, high-pitched and excited. "Jack! Welcome! Please come in!"

He steps inside, and I can't resist drinking in every detail of him. He looks infuriatingly perfect—his dark hair slightly messy, his bright eyes sparkling with life. The blue sweater he's wearing fits snugly over his muscular form, causing my throat to go dry.

Out of the blue, a memory flashes through my mind:

Felix, standing in our bedroom doorway, his face a mask of feigned remorse. "It didn't mean anything, Jenn. You have to believe me."

The echo of my own broken sobs rings in my ears, and I have to shake my head to dispel the image.

As Jack takes in all the Christmas decorations around him, his eyes widen in awe for a moment. He almost looks like a boy, and I hate how my heart responds to that image. No. I won't let myself be fooled again.

“Wow. This is... amazing. You've really outdone yourself.”

His rich, warm voice, reminiscent of aged whiskey, stirs a storm inside me. Anger, pain, and frustration swirl together into a toxic mixture that has been brewing for weeks. Underneath it all, there’s a traitorous spark of desire I can’t seem to extinguish.

Unwelcome memories flood my mind once again. Only this time, my mind brings back his touch on my skin, his lips on my body, the way he made me feel... I clench my fists so hard that my nails dig into my palms as I try to push those images away.

In an instant, Jack's eyes flick over to me as if sensing my gaze. They widen in recognition and then darken with an intensity that steals my breath and freezes me in place.

Anna says something to him, but he doesn't seem to hear her. His focus is entirely on me as he crosses the room, each step sending jolts of electricity through me.

He stops right in front of me, close enough that I can smell his cologne—that irresistible combination of spice and pine that has been haunting my dreams.

”Princess,” he breathes, the nickname sliding off his tongue like a delicate touch.

That one word shatters my paralysis. Rage takes over, burning hot and fierce. How dare he? How dare he use that name, implying that there was ever any intimacy between us when it was all a lie?

Without thinking, I grab a nearby cocktail and fling it at him. The crimson liquid splatters across his perfectly chiseled features, dripping down his chin and staining his blue sweater. “Don't you dare 'Princess' me,” I seethe. “You lying, cheating bastard.”

Jack blinks, droplets clinging to his long lashes, his

expression a mix of shock and... something else I can't quite decipher.

Anna gasps, her hand flying to her mouth in disbelief.

Meanwhile, I stand there with an empty glass still clutched in my trembling hand, my chest heaving with emotions towards the man who shattered my heart.

The Christmas lights twinkle innocently above us, providing a stark contrast to the tension crackling in the air. As the red liquid slowly drips down Jack's jawline, a part of me feels satisfied for standing up to him, while another part mourns the connection that never truly existed between us.

Peter bursts in from the kitchen, eyes wide as he takes in the scene. "What the—"

Anna rushes to my side, her jingle bell earrings tinkling discordantly. "Jenn, what's wrong? What happened?"

I can't tear my gaze from Jack's face. His eyes burn into mine, unblinking. He doesn't flinch, doesn't back down. It only stokes the inferno raging inside me.

"What's wrong?" I laugh, a harsh, bitter sound that scrapes my throat. "What's wrong is that you've invited a lying, cheating bastard into your home."

I turn to Peter, my voice dripping with venom. "You should know, Peter. Your colleague here? He's the worst kind of man there is."

Peter's brow furrows in confusion. He grabs a handful of napkins, offering them to Jack with a mumbled, "I'm so sorry."

The gesture ignites a fresh wave of fury within me. Sorry? He's sorry? To him?

"Don't apologize to him," I spit. "He's the one who should be sorry."

Anna's grip on my arm tightens. "Jenn, honey, what are you talking about? How do you know Jack?"

I huff out a breath, my lips curling into a cynical smirk. “Oh, we go way back. All the way to last month, in fact.”

I turn to Anna. “Remember that guy from the club?” The one who made me feel things I'd never felt before? The one who tied me up in the stairwell and fucked me senseless, I scream in my head.

Anna's eyes widen, her hand flying to her mouth. “No, you mean...”

“That's right,” I nod, my gaze sliding back to Jack.

He's still watching me, his expression unreadable as he dabs at his face with the napkins. “Meet your perfect match, Anna. The Christmas Prince himself.”

Anna gasps, her head whipping between Jack and me. “But... but that can't be right. Jack's not—”

“Not what?” I interrupt, my voice rising. “Not the type to seduce a woman and then go home to his girlfriend? Not the kind of guy who'd make you feel special, wanted, or desired, only to turn around and call another woman 'Honey'?”

The words pour out of me, a torrent of pain and anger I've been holding back for a month. I can feel the others' stunned gazes, but I can't stop. Won't stop. The dam has broken, and I'm drowning in the flood.

“Well, newsflash, Anna. He is exactly that type. So congratulations on your matchmaking skills. You've managed to find the one man in New York who could make me feel even more worthless than I already did.”

I finish, chest heaving, tears pricking at the corners of my eyes. The silence that follows is deafening, broken only by the cheerful tinkling of “Jingle Bells” from some godforsaken decoration.

And through it all, Jack just stands there, his eyes never leaving mine, a storm brewing in their depths.

Suddenly he breaks his motionless stance and turns to

Anna, his eyes softening in a way that makes my stomach churn. “Anna, could I have a moment with the princess?”

Princess. That damn endearment again. I cringe, scowling at the warmth that threatens to bloom in my chest. Get it together, Jenn. He's playing you. Again.

Anna's eyes narrow with suspicion, and I can't help but feel a surge of warmth towards her as she steps between us. “Is what Jennifer says true? Did you deceive her like a heartless bastard?” Her voice is firm, laced with barely contained anger. “Don't even think about messing with me. Tell the truth.”

I can't hide the smirk that tugs at my lips. *Got you now, asshole.*

But Jack remains unfazed. His gaze remains steady as he replies, “Yes, I'm the guy from the club last month. But there seems to have been a big misunderstanding that I need to clear up with your friend.”

Then he leans in and whispers something to Anna that I can't hear, and suddenly she looks different. Her face loses its anger and changes to something else.

“Peter,” she calls out. “Let's give them some privacy. We'll be in the kitchen if you need us, Jenn.”

What. The. Actual. Hell.

“Anna!” I shout, panic rising in my throat. “You can't be serious. He's lying.”

But she just turns and walks away with a small smile on her face. “Trust me, sweetie. Listen to him.” And then they disappear into the kitchen together.

I stand there in disbelief, feeling utterly betrayed by Anna's sudden change of heart. *How could she switch sides so easily? What did he say to her?*

Before I can process this new betrayal, Jack shifts his focus back to me. The intensity in his eyes hits me like a tangible force, instantly transporting me to that stairwell.

No. I shake my head, trying to clear the fog of desire that threatens to cloud my judgment. I won't let him manipulate me again.

"Whatever game you're playing," I hiss, backing away, "I'm not interested."

But Jack doesn't back down. He takes a step closer, his voice low and husky. "No games, Princess. Just the truth. If you'll let me explain."

My back hits the wall, and suddenly he's there, caging me in with his arms. The scent of him—spice, pine, and man—overwhelms my senses. I'm trembling, caught between the urge to knee him in the groin and the traitorous desire to pull him closer.

"Why should I believe anything you say?" I whisper, hating how breathless I sound.

A dark intensity fills his eyes, and for a moment, I feel the familiar pull of desire that consumed us both that night.

"Because," he murmurs, his lips mere inches from mine, "I haven't been able to stop thinking about you since that night. And I'm pretty sure you haven't been able to stop thinking about me either."

I scoff, trying to ignore the way my heart races at his nearness. "Thinking about you? Please. I erased you from my memory the moment I caught you with your girlfriend."

My words come out harsh, but I don't care because he crushed my last bit of hope in finding an honest man.

"So stop with the lies," I snap, pushing against his chest. "You're only upset because you lost your easy lay."

His hand shoots out and grips my chin, forcing me to look up at him. "Don't ever call yourself that. What we had that night was real. Every. Damn. Second."

I scowl, trying to ignore the shiver his touch sends through me. "Real? My ass."

The sudden smirk tugging at the corner of his lips catches me off guard. "Speaking of your ass," he murmurs, "it's one of the many things I can't forget about you. Along with those little sounds you made when I—"

"Shut up," I hiss, heat flooding my cheeks.

We fall into a tense silence, our eyes locked in a wordless battle. There's something in his gaze that throws me off-balance, something that makes my breath catch in my throat.

"I looked for you that night," he says softly. "When you didn't come back, I searched the entire club. Three times."

For a split second, I almost believe him. Almost. But I've learned the hard way not to trust sweet words and intense gazes.

"How sweet," I drawl, sarcasm dripping from every word. "Did your girlfriend help with the search party?"

"She probably wouldn't have," he says slowly, "if I had a girlfriend. Which I don't."

"Liar." I try to break away from him. But his arms are like iron bars, keeping me caged against the wall.

"Jennifer. Please, just listen to me."

"Listen and succumb to your lies again? No thanks."

"Dammit," he growls, his face inches from mine. "What happened between us that night wasn't fake. It was real, raw, and fucking incredible."

"How can you say that after what I saw and heard with my own eyes and ears?"

Confusion crosses his face as he furrows his brow. "What exactly did you see and hear that convinced you I have a girlfriend?"

The question sets me off again. He thinks I'm the fool here? Fine. Let's spell it out for him.

"You want a play-by-play?" I snarl, my voice dripping with venom. "After our... encounter, I ran into Anna. Told her about the nice man I'd met." I laugh bitterly at the memory. "Then I went to find you, like you'd asked. And where do I find you? At the bar, with your back turned to me."

Jack's grip on my arm loosens slightly, but he doesn't let go. His intense gaze remains fixed on me as I recount what happened next.

"That's when this gorgeous blonde walks up to you," I say, the scene playing out in my mind like a twisted movie. "She asks why you weren't home. And then you called her 'Honey' in that adoring voice of yours and told her you were sorry and that something came up and time slipped away from you."

I look at him, daring him to talk his way out of it. But instead of looking caught, his expression is painful. He curses under his breath, then reaches out to tuck a lock of hair behind my ear. The tenderness of the gesture only adds to the turmoil of emotions inside me.

"Just to clarify," he speaks softly. "You think I have a girlfriend because I called her 'Honey'?"

When I nod, he sighs deeply before speaking again, "The blonde woman you saw? She's my stepsister."

I blink, struggling to process his words. "Your... stepsister?"

"Yes." His eyes never leave mine. "Tall, curvy, leggy blonde? Blue eyes? Looks like she could be a model."

His description matches perfectly, and I nod in disbelief.

"That's her," Jack states with a slight smirk. "My stepsister."

"Bullshit. Why would you call your stepsister 'Honey'? That's just weird."

His smirk widens as he grabs my wrists and holds them

between us. "It would be strange," he admits, "if that wasn't her actual name."

I freeze, my mind reeling. "Her... her name is Honey?"

A twinkle of amusement sparkles in his eyes. "Honey Daniels. My stepsister."

I stare at him as my skepticism kicks in, refusing to let go of the hurt and anger I've been holding onto for weeks.

"Right," I scoff, pulling my arms free and crossing them in front of me. "And I'm the Queen of England."

His jaw clenches, creating a defined line along his square jaw. "Need more proof? Fine."

He takes a step back and quickly fishes out his phone from his pocket. I watch as he furiously taps the screen, then holds it up for me to see. The speaker crackles to life as it rings.

"Answer the damn phone," he mutters under his breath, but it goes to voicemail. He groans in frustration, his hand running through his dark hair.

I raise an eyebrow skeptically, ready to throw another snarky comment his way when a woman's voice fills the air.

"Hey, you've reached Honey! I'm probably off doing something fabulous, so leave a message if you want me to grace you with a callback. Ciao!"

My stomach drops at the sound of her voice. It's the same blonde from the bar who Jack claimed is his stepsister. My mind races to make sense of this new information, but my cynicism kicks in as a defense mechanism.

"So what?" I manage, trying to keep my voice steady. Even as the words leave my mouth, I can't ignore the small glimmer of hope that's started to take root. Could it really be true? Could he be telling the truth about Honey?

My mind races, the logical part of me still clinging to the cynicism that has protected me for so long. This could all be an elaborate ruse, another cruel trick to get me to let my guard down. The memory of Felix's betrayal flashes through my mind, a bitter reminder of the pain I've endured.

I chance a glance at Jack, and the frustration and determination I see in his expression gives me pause. This isn't the smooth-talking charmer from the club – this is a man who seems genuinely invested in proving his sincerity. But can I really trust that? After everything I've been through, how can I be sure he's not just another skilled manipulator?

"You could have set that up," I argue, the words sounding hollow even to my own ears. "It doesn't prove anything."

He looks frustrated and determined all at once. “I'll prove you wrong, Princess.”

The conviction in his voice sends a shiver down my spine. Part of me wants to believe him, to let go of my cynicism and take a chance. But the memory of past pain lingers in my mind, like a shadow that follows me everywhere I go.

I take a deep breath, trying to calm myself. “Look, we should probably get to dinner. Anna put a lot of effort into this, and I don't want to ruin it any more than I already have. I can be civil for a few hours. But after that, we go our separate ways. For good.”

Jack steps closer, his cologne engulfing me once again. “That's not happening,” he murmurs, his voice low and intense. “I'm not letting you walk away from this... from us.”

I prepare to argue back when Anna's head pops around the corner, her eyes wide with curiosity. “Everything alright here?”

I plaster on a fake smile, ignoring the way my heart races at Jack's proximity. “Just peachy, Anna. We're coming,” I say through gritted teeth before pushing past him and making my way towards the dining room.

Anna and Peter's gazes flit between us, their eyes filled

with unspoken questions as we enter. Before I can say anything, Jack speaks.

"Anna, Peter, this table looks incredible. I can't wait to taste everything."

I roll my eyes. "Smooth talker," I mutter under my breath.

Anna comes my way and gently but firmly guides me to a corner of the room. "Spill," she whispers, her eyes wide with curiosity. "How did it go?"

I snort, crossing my arms. "Oh, it went great. Prince Charming over there tried to convince me his 'girlfriend' is actually his stepsister. Named Honey, of all things. Can you believe it?"

To my surprise, Anna's brow furrows. "Well... why couldn't that be true?"

I stare at her, disbelief coursing through me. "Are you kidding me? It's the oldest trick in the book, Anna. Next, he'll be telling me he has a bridge to sell me in Brooklyn."

Anna's lips purse, her expression thoughtful. "I don't know, Jenn. Maybe you should give him a chance to explain."

"I've given him enough chances," I glance over at Jack, who is chatting with Peter and looking far too at ease for my liking. "I'm going to endure this dinner, and then we're done. For good."

We take our seats, Jack sitting across from me. His gaze focused on mine, and I quickly look away, focusing on the appetizer in front of me.

"I have an idea," Anna says, and I can see the enthusiasm in her eyes. "Let's all share something we're grateful for."

I can't help but snort. "It's not Thanksgiving, Anna."

"Jennifer," she scolds me, her tone sharp. "Don't be rude."

Heat rises to my cheeks as she begins talking about her gratitude for friends and family. Peter follows suit, his words sweet and genuine. Then it's Jack's turn, and I braced myself.

“I'm thankful for unexpected encounters.” He looks directly at me. “The kind that shakes up your world and makes you see things differently.”

For a moment, I’m transported back to the club, feeling the electricity of our first touch. I angrily stab at my salad while repeating in my head: Don't fall for it, Jenn. He's playing you.

“Jack,” Anna interrupts my thoughts. “Tell us more about your volunteer work with the youth organization. It sounds fascinating.”

I can't resist looking up, curiosity getting the best of me, only to see Jack's face soften and a warmth enter his eyes.

“It's close to my heart,” he admits quietly but passionately. “My father passed away when I was three, and I know how much having a positive male role model can mean to a kid.”

Jack's eyes shine with genuine passion as he talks about the kids he mentors. For a moment, I'm taken back to my own childhood:

A much younger me, sitting alone on a playground swing, watching other kids laugh with their fathers. The ache in my chest, a longing for something I'd never had.

I blink, surprised by the sudden lump in my throat. Maybe Jack and I have more in common than I thought.

As Jack regales Anna and Peter with another anecdote from his youth work, I find myself watching him intently. His eyes light up as he speaks, his hands gesturing animatedly. I’m struck by how different he seems from the smooth operator I met at the club.

“So there's Tommy, covered head to toe in flour, looking like a ghost,” Jack chuckles, his deep laugh sending an involuntary shiver down my spine. “And he just looks at me and says, 'I think we need more eggs.'”

Anna and Peter burst into laughter, and I can't help the small smile that tugs at my lips. There's a warmth in Jack's voice when he talks about these kids, a genuine care that I hadn't expected. It's... endearing, and I find myself wondering if this is the real Jack—not the suave charmer from the club, but this passionate, caring man.

As Peter launches into a story of his own misadventures in baking, I notice Jack's gaze flick towards me. Our eyes meet for a brief moment, and the intensity I see there makes my breath catch. It's the same look he gave me that night in the stairwell, a mixture of desire and something deeper, something that scared me then and, if I'm honest, still scares me now.

I quickly look away, focusing on my plate. My mind is whirling. How can this be the same man I thought had played me? The Jack I see tonight fits so poorly with the image I’ve built up in my head over the past month. This man is funny, intelligent, and clearly devoted to his work. The way Anna and Peter have taken to him so quickly... it’s hard to reconcile with the idea of him being a player.

But then I remember Honey, the blonde at the bar. Jack's explanation about her being his stepsister nags at me. Could it be true? The cynical part of me wants to dismiss it outright, but another part—a part I've been trying to ignore—whispers that maybe, just maybe, I've misjudged him.

“Jenn?” Anna's voice cuts through my thoughts. “You okay? You've been quiet.”

I blink, realizing I've been lost in my own head. “Sorry, just... thinking.”

“About what?” Jack asks, his voice soft and curious.

Our eyes meet again, and for a moment, I consider telling

him. Laying out all my doubts, my fears, my confusion. But the vulnerability terrifies me, so I deflect.

"Just wondering how you managed to survive that baking disaster," I say, forcing a light tone. "Sounds like you're a menace in the kitchen"

He grins, accepting my deflection with grace. "Oh, you have no idea. I'm a disaster with anything more complicated than a microwave."

As the conversation flows on, I can't shake the feeling that I'm standing on a precipice. On one side is the safety of my cynicism, my carefully constructed walls. On the other... well, that's the terrifying part. I don't know what's on the other side. But as I watch Jack laugh with Anna and Peter, I think back to the day I met Felix, his charming smile and smooth words. "You're different from other girls, Jenn. Special." The same words he'd probably used on his secretary.

I grip my glass tighter, trying to quell the rising panic. But Jack isn't Felix. Is he?

I force a smile as Jack finishes his story about Tommy, trying to push away the warm feeling in my chest. His passion is... intoxicating. No, stop it, Jenn. You're not falling for this again.

"The kids adore you, Jack," Peter exclaims, his eyes shining with admiration.

Jack chuckles. "Look who's talking. I swear, from the moment you walked in the kids liked you. And now everytime you talk about Anna, and the fun things you do, the kids hang on your lips."

Anna smiles, her hand finding Peter's on the table. "Oh, stop it," she giggles, but the rosy flush on her cheeks gives away her happiness.

"It's truly heartwarming," Jack says, his gaze sweeping

over the couple. “To see such genuine love between two people. How did you two meet?”

As Anna begins to share their romantic story, her eyes light up with joy. But as I listen to her words, a familiar ache fills my chest. It's the longing for something I'm not sure I'll ever have.

“I just wish my best friend could experience that kind of love.” Anna sighs, shooting a pointed look in my direction. “Jennifer hasn't had much luck in the romance department.”

Heat rushes to my face as I shoot Anna a glare.

“Anna!” I hiss, feeling mortified and vulnerable under their pitying gazes. “That's not appropriate dinner conversation.”

But Jack leans forward, his eyes focused on me. “Really? And what was Jennifer's worst relationship, according to you?”

“Oh, Felix was the absolute worst,” Anna laments with a sympathetic tone, and I shrink into my chair.

“He swept Jenn off her feet, you know? All grand gestures and promises of forever.”

I bite my lip until I taste copper. Images of Felix’s charming smile flash through my mind, quickly followed by the horror that still churns my stomach.

“They were together for two years,” Anna continues on, oblivious to my discomfort. “Jenn truly believed he was The One. They even talked about getting married.”

Jack's eyes lock onto mine from across the table, his expression intense and impossible to read.

“But then,” Anna lowers her voice to a whisper, “Jenn decided to surprise him one day by coming home early. And well...”

Not wanting to hear more, I push away from the table with a screech of my chair against the floor. “I need some fresh air," I mutter, quickly escaping the dining room and ignoring the concerned calls behind me.

The cool night air hits my face as I step onto the concrete of the backyard, and I greedily gulp it down, trying to calm my racing heart. Footsteps approach, and I tense, expecting Anna's apologetic babble. But the presence behind me is too strong, too intense to be my well-meaning friend.

Keeping my gaze fixed on the cold concrete walls, I speak without turning. "If you've come to offer sympathy, don't bother. I've had enough of that for a lifetime."

Jack's body radiates heat like a furnace as he moves closer, and I have to stop myself from leaning into his warmth.

"I didn't come here to pity you," he murmurs. "I came to tell you that Felix was an idiot."

"Well, thanks, but you have no idea," I retort, my voice shaky.

"I know what you're feeling. I've been there," he says softly, his tone tinged with pain. "My wife of five years… she cheated on me. On our anniversary, of all days."

His words hit me like a punch to the gut. I turn, searching his face for any sign of deceit, but all I see is honesty and raw anguish. "It's unforgivable," he continues, his voice hardening. "If you're unhappy in a relationship, have the decency to end it. Cheating… it's a cowardly way out."

The conviction in his voice leaves me stunned. It's like looking into a mirror, seeing my own hurt and anger reflected back at me. For the first time since that night at the club, I feel a spark of something dangerous. Hope.

I take in his features, the moonlight casting shadows over his face, emphasizing the tension in his jaw and the slight furrow between his brows. In that moment, I see beyond his charming façade and catch a glimpse of a man who might understand the scars I carry better than I'd like to admit.

Meeting Jack's intense gaze, filled with raw emotion, makes me swallow hard. It would be so easy to give in, to let myself fall. But the memory of Felix's betrayal rises up like acid in my throat, a painful reminder of why I've kept my defenses up for so long.

"I don't know what to believe anymore," I confess, my voice barely audible over the rustling leaves.

Jack steps closer, his warmth enveloping me. "Then don't believe," he murmurs, his breath teasing my skin. "Just feel."

His words are tempting, but my mind is still torn between doubt and desire.

"How can I trust my feelings when they've led me astray before?" I ask.

Jack's jaw clenches, but then his expression softens. He reaches out, fingers ghosting along my cheek. "It was not a move, Jennifer. What happened between us that night… I've never experienced anything like it."

The intensity in his eyes, the slight tremor in his touch… it feels real. Dangerously, intoxicatingly real.

"I want to believe you," I whisper, surprised by my own honesty. "But I've been burned before. Badly."

Jack nods, understanding in his eyes. "I'm scared too," he confesses. "Scared that I'll mess this up, that I'll lose you before I even have a chance to get to know you."

His words hang in the air, heavy with promise and possibility. For a moment, I let myself imagine what it would be like to trust him, to let down my walls.

"I can't promise I won't make mistakes," Jack continues. "But I can promise that I'll always be honest with you. That I'll never intentionally hurt you. And that I'll do everything in my power to prove that your trust in me isn't misplaced."

Tears prick at the corners of my eyes, overwhelmed by the sincerity in his voice. “I want to believe that,” I whisper. “I want to trust you.”

His fingers brush my cheek again, and I lean into his touch, the warmth of his skin both thrilling and terrifying. For a moment, I let myself imagine what it would be like to give in, to trust him, to feel…

Then reality crashes back. I jerk away, heart pounding. “I'm sorry,” I mutter, wrapping my arms around myself. “I can't… I just can't.”

I brace myself for anger or frustration, but Jack's voice is soft, almost tender. “Okay. Then I'll wait.”

My head snaps up, eyes wide with disbelief. “What?”

A small smile plays at the corners of his mouth. “You heard me, Princess. I'll wait until you're ready.”

Before I can process this, he gestures towards the house. “We should probably head back inside. Don't want to worry our hosts.”

I nod, my mind whirling with confusion and surprise. My feet move mechanically as we make our way back to the house, my thoughts still caught up in his unexpected response.

As we step through the doorway, Anna rushes towards me, her face a picture of concern. “Jenn, I'm so sorry. I was just-”

I raise my hand, cutting her off mid-sentence. A small, reassuring smile tugs at my lips. “It’s okay. I know you meant well.”

Eager to change the subject, I ask, “So what's for dessert?”

Anna's eyes light up, and her lips curl into a proud grin. “My famous cheesecake.”

"Oh I can't wait to taste that," Jack chimes in, brushing past us on his way to the dining room.

We gather around the table, forks poised over slices of Anna's renowned cheesecake. Jack takes a bite and his eyes widen in delight. He swallows and launches into a story about a disastrous baking attempt that has us all in stitches. His eyes crinkle at the corners when he laughs, and I find myself drawn in by his animated gestures and playful tone.

"Oh, come on," I argue, surprising myself with how easily I fall into the banter. "You can't possibly think cheese-cake beats a good old-fashioned chocolate cake."

Jack gasps in mock horror. "Blasphemy! Cheesecake is clearly superior in every way."

As we playfully debate dessert merits, a memory flashes through my mind. The bar, that night. How effortlessly we'd fallen into conversation, trading quips and stories like we'd known each other for years. It was one of the reasons I'd trusted him; let my guard down. And let him fuck me sense-less in that stairwell.

Heat floods my cheeks as memories wash over me. The way he'd tied my wrists together, his lips hot on my neck, his hands... God, his hands. I shift in my seat, acutely aware of his presence across the table. And to my own amazement, I find myself wishing he could do it all over again.

When the night winds down, dessert plates cleared and conversation ebbing. I find myself lingering, reluctant to leave the warmth of the evening. Jack's presence, once so unsettling, has become... comfortable. He didn't push, didn't try to charm his way past my defenses. Instead, he just was. Funny, passionate about his work, quick with a self-depre-cating joke.

I hate to admit it, but I liked the man I saw tonight. And

his explanation about Honey nags at me, a persistent whisper of possibility.

"Thank you both for an amazing dinner," Jack says, his smile genuine as he embraces Anna and shakes Peter's hand.

"What are your plans for Christmas, Jack?" Anna asks, ever the hostess.

Jack's eyes crinkle at the corners. "Christmas Day is for family," he says. "But the second day? That's all mine. Pajamas, movies, and absolutely zero responsibilities."

The image of Jack lounging in pajamas, hair tousled from sleep, flashes unbidden through my mind. I push it away, cheeks heating.

Then he's in front of me, emerald orbs holding mine captive. "It was good to see you, Jennifer." And with that, he turns, leaving me staring after him as Peter walks to the front door. Anna sidles up beside me, a knowing smile playing on her lips.

"You two had some serious chemistry going on," she says.

I scoff, falling back on cynicism like a security blanket. "Please. The man's nothing but trouble."

But even as the words leave my mouth, a traitorous voice whispers in the back of my mind.

Maybe. But what delicious trouble he could be.

Chapter 8

Jennifer

I toss the damp dish towel onto the counter, surveying my spotless kitchen with a mix of pride and frustration. It's barely noon on Boxing Day, and I've already cleaned every surface in my apartment twice. Anything to keep my hands busy and my mind from wandering to dangerous territory.

As I move to the living room, my eyes land on the small Christmas tree in the corner. It's a pitiful thing, really—a two-foot artificial pine I bought on clearance years ago. I never bothered with many decorations, but one ornament catches my eye.

It's a delicate glass heart, cracked down the middle and held together with gold paint. A kintsugi heart, Anna had called it when she gave it to me last Christmas. "To remind you that even broken things can be beautiful," she'd said with a sad smile, knowing how raw my wounds still were from Felix's betrayal.

I reach out, my fingers tracing the golden fissure. For the past year, this ornament has been a perfect representation of my cynicism about love — broken, scarred, and pieced back together, but never quite the same.

But now, as I study it, I see it differently. The golden lines aren't just scars; they're a roadmap of resilience. The heart isn't weaker for having been broken; it's stronger, more beautiful for having survived.

Is that what Jack sees when he looks at me? Not someone broken beyond repair, but someone made stronger by their experiences?

I shake my head, trying to dispel the dangerous yearning blooming in my chest. But as I turn away from the tree, I can't help but glance back at the ornament. For the first time in a long time, I don't see it as a symbol of my broken heart, but as a promise of what could be.

With a sigh, I sink onto the couch, exhaustion seeping into my bones. Those thoughts I've been desperately avoiding crash over me like a tidal wave.

Jack.

I close my eyes, but it only makes his image more vivid. Those forest-green eyes, crinkling at the corners as he laughed. The way his stained sweater stretched across his broad shoulders as he reached for the salt shaker. The low timbre of his voice as he murmured, "I'll wait."

"He's just a man," I mutter, fingers digging into the couch cushions. "Nothing special. Nothing worth risking your heart over."

But my traitorous body disagrees. Heat pools low in my belly as memories of that night in the stairwell flash through my mind. The way his hands gripped my hips and how his lips trailed fire down my neck. The delicious friction as he played with my—

"Stop it!" I hiss, jumping to my feet. I pace the living room, trying to outrun my own desires. But it's futile. With every step, new fantasies bloom.

Jack, pressing me against the bookshelf, his breath hot on my ear as he whispers filthy promises.

Jack, sprawled on my bed, eyes dark with want as I straddle him.

Jack, his fingers tangled in my hair as I take him in my mouth, his groans of pleasure sending shivers down my spine.

I collapse back onto the couch, breath coming in short pants. This is madness. I barely know him. He could break my heart just like—

But a small voice whispers, *What if he's not? What if this time is different?*

I groan, burying my face in a throw pillow. It's been so long since I've felt this way—this intoxicating mix of desire and possibility. Part of me wants to run to protect myself from the potential pain.

But a larger part, growing stronger by the minute, wants to dive in headfirst. To feel Jack's hands on my skin again, to lose myself in his kisses, to explore every inch of him until we're both breathless and sated.

A sharp knock jolts me from my heated reverie. I freeze, heart hammering against my ribs. Who could it be? Jack? No, he doesn't even know where I live. I rise on shaky legs, smoothing my hair and praying my flushed cheeks aren't too obvious.

I open the door and nearly choke on my own tongue. It's her. The stunning blonde from the bar. Jack's... girlfriend? My stomach twists with a sickening combination of dread and jealousy, but before I can slam the door shut, she flashes me a megawatt smile that catches me off guard.

"Hi! I'm Honey Daniels. Jack's stepsister. Can I come in? I promise I'm not crazy; I just really need to talk to you."

She doesn't wait for an answer, breezing past me in a

cloud of expensive perfume. I blink, trying to catch up with the unexpected turn of events, my mind racing to make sense of the situation.

"I... what?"

Honey turns to face me, her blue eyes burning with determination. "I know what you're thinking, but please hear me out. Jack is really my stepbrother. When I heard what happened at the club, I had to set things straight."

My brain goes haywire. She really is his stepsister? Not his girlfriend?

"I mean, don't get me wrong," Honey says, wrinkling her nose. "Jack's a total dreamboat, but ew. In no universe would I ever be interested in him like that. It'd be like making out with a golden retriever."

I cannot help but chuckle at the image she is painting.

Honey grins at me, her playful demeanor putting me more at ease.

"Seriously, though. Give the guy a chance. He's been a miserable, moody ass of a stepbrother this past month. You should've seen him after his ex—a total bitch, by the way—broke his heart. But Jack? He'd never cheat. Sure, he's a charming bastard, but he's loyal to the bone."

Her defense of his character is compelling, and I find myself wanting to give him the benefit of the doubt. But cynicism has become second nature to me.

"If he's so great," I say sarcastically, raising an eyebrow, "why isn't he here defending himself?"

The words slip out before I can stop them, and I instantly regret it. It's not fair, and I know it. Jack did try to explain at the dinner, his eyes pleading with me to understand. But I'd been too hurt and too scared to listen.

Honey narrows her eyes, her lips pursing into a thin line.

"He already did, sweetheart. But you wouldn't believe him, would you? That's why I'm here."

Heat creeps up my neck, but I can't back down now. "Oh, so he sent his sister to fight his battles? How chivalrous."

"Please," Honey scoffs, rolling her eyes. "As if Jack could make me do anything I didn't want to. I'm here because I care about the idiot, and I'm tired of watching him mope around like a kicked puppy."

I cross my arms, trying to ignore the way my heart clenches at the image. "Well, maybe he should've thought of that before—"

"Before what?" Honey interrupts, her voice sharp. "Before his well-meaning but admittedly impulsive stepsister caused a misunderstanding? Or before he tried to prove to you that he's not the asshole you seem determined to paint him as?"

Her words hit me like a slap, and I falter. Honey's right, and we both know it. But admitting that means facing the possibility that I've been wrong. That I've been pushing away something—someone—that could be amazing.

Honey's expression softens, and she takes a step closer. "Look, I get it. You're scared. But Jack? He's the real deal. And I think you know that, or you wouldn't be fighting so hard against it."

A laugh bubbles up in my throat, unexpected and slightly hysterical. "God, do you ever let up?"

"Nope," Honey grins, popping the 'p'. "It's part of my charm."

And just like that, the tension dissipates. We both burst into laughter, the absurdity of the situation finally hitting us. The gorgeous blonde who I thought was my almost-lover's girlfriend is now lecturing me in my living room.

As our giggles subside, I find myself studying Honey.

There's something refreshing about her bluntness, her unwavering loyalty to her stepbrother. It's a far cry from the cattiness I've come to expect from other women.

“You know,” I say, wiping tears of mirth from my eyes, “you're not at all what I expected.”

Honey quirks an eyebrow. “Let me guess. You thought I'd be some brainless bimbo hanging off Jack's arm?”

I wince but nod. “Well, um, yes, something like that. I'm sorry, I shouldn't have—”

“Please,” Honey waves off my apology. “I've heard worse. Besides, I kind of like you, Jennifer. You've got spunk.”

“Thanks,” I smile, surprised to find I mean it. “You're not so bad yourself.”

Honey's eyes sparkle with mischief. “So, now that we've established I'm not trying to steal your man, can we talk about how you're going to make it up to Jack? Because let me tell you, honey, that man is head over heels for you.”

My heart skips a beat, and I try to ignore the thrill that runs through me at her words. “I... I don't know if I'm ready for that.”

“Bullshit,” Honey says, but there's no heat behind it. “You're ready. You're just scared.”

Honey's eyes soften, a hint of sadness creeping into her voice. “You know, Jack told me about your ex. How he cheated on you.”

My breath catches in my throat. I hadn't expected Jack to share that with anyone, let alone his stepsister.

“Yeah, well,” I mutter, looking away. “It's not exactly something I like to broadcast.”

“I get it,” Honey nods. “But you know what? I think that's why you and Jack have been so nice about this whole mess. You both know how much it hurts.”

I raise an eyebrow. “Nice? I wouldn't exactly call running away 'nice.'”

Honey lets out a sharp laugh. “Trust me, sweetheart. You two are saints compared to what I would've done.” Her blue eyes gleam with a wicked light. “If I'd caught my man cheating? Let's just say his balls would've made excellent Christmas ornaments.”

I can't help but snort at the vivid image. “God, you're terrible.”

“I prefer 'creatively vindictive,'“ Honey grins. Then her expression turns serious again. “Look, all I'm asking is for you to give Jack a chance. That's it.”

I chew my lip, teetering on the edge of a decision that could change everything. Part of me still wants to run to protect myself from potential heartbreak. But then Honey's voice cuts through my swirling thoughts.

“You know, sometimes the biggest regrets in life are the chances we didn't take.”

Her words hit like a sucker punch to the gut. I think about the past year and how I've hidden behind my walls, pushing away anyone who tried to get close. How I've been so focused on protecting myself that I've missed out on actually living.

And suddenly, I'm tired.

Tired of being afraid.

Tired of letting my past dictate my future.

“You're right,” I whisper, the words feeling foreign on my tongue. “I've been... I've been hiding.”

Honey's face lights up, but she doesn't say anything, letting me work through my thoughts.

“Maybe it's time I took a chance.”

The words are barely out of my mouth before I'm asking, “Do you have Jack's address?”

Honey's triumphant grin could light up Times Square. “Honey, I thought you'd never ask.”

Before I can process what's happening, she launches herself at me, enveloping me in a tight hug that knocks the breath from my lungs.

“Thank God!” she exclaims, squeezing me tighter. “I was running out of sisterly wisdom. Another minute and I'd have resorted to quoting fortune cookies.”

I laugh, the sound muffled against her shoulder.

“Coffee?” I offer, suddenly aware of how surreal this situation is.

“Yep, I live on caffeine,” Honey grins, following me into the kitchen.

As I busy myself with the coffee maker, Honey's gaze sweeps the room, landing on a bottle on the counter. Her eyebrow quirks up, a mischievous glint in her eye.

“Jack Daniels, huh? Didn't peg you for a whiskey girl.”

Heat creeps up my neck. “It's... a guilty pleasure.”

Honey's laugh is warm and rich. “Oh honey, this is too perfect. You know that's Jack's full name, right? Jack Daniels?”

I nearly drop the mug I'm holding. “You're kidding.”

“Nope,” she pops the 'p' again, grinning. “Must be fate.”

I can't help but laugh, the absurdity of it all hitting me. Jack Daniels, indeed. The universe has a twisted sense of humor.

As we sip our coffee, conversation flows easily. Honey regales me with embarrassing stories from Jack's childhood, and I find myself warming to her brash honesty and wicked sense of humor.

“Well,” Honey says finally, draining the last of her coffee. “As much as I'd love to stay and chat, I've got a hot date with a trashy romance novel.”

She stands but pauses at the door. “Oh, and Jennifer? Wear that dress. You know the one from the club; he liked it a lot.”

I feel my cheeks flush. Honey winks, then she's gone in a cloud of perfume and possibility.

I sink onto the couch, my head spinning. Jack's stepsister. Not his girlfriend. The relief is almost dizzying, but it's quickly replaced by a gnawing anxiety.

What now?

I close my eyes, trying to sort through the whirlwind of emotions. Part of me wants to rush to Jack's apartment right now, to throw myself into his arms and forget about all the misunderstandings. But the cynical voice in my head, the one that's kept me safe for so long, pipes up.

Are you really going to trust him so easily? After Felix?

I twist my hands in my lap, torn. “It's different,” I whisper to myself. “Jack's different.”

Is he? Or are you just desperate to believe that?

The memory of Jack's eyes, warm and sincere as he told me he'd wait, flashes through my mind. But so does the image of Felix, his face a mask of remorse as he swore it would never happen again.

I stand up, pacing the living room. Honey's words echo in my mind: “Sometimes the biggest regrets in life are the chances we didn't take.”

“Okay,” I say out loud, my voice shaky but determined. “Okay, I'm doing this.”

A minute later, I stand in front of my closet, debating what to wear. My heart races as I slip into the dress, the fabric cool against my heated skin. The silky material clings to my curves, reminding me of the night at the club when Jack's eyes couldn't leave me. I take a deep breath, steadying myself against the rush of anticipation coursing through my veins.

Before I can lose my nerve, I grab my keys and coat and head for the door. The words echo in my mind, drowning out the doubts that threaten to overwhelm me.

A few moments later, I find myself in a cab, heading towards Jack's apartment. My heart races, a mix of anticipation and nervousness coursing through me. But as I picture the kintsugi heart, I feel a sense of calm settle over me. Whatever happens, I know I'm strong enough to handle it.

Half an hour later, the cab pulls up to a sleek apartment building, all glass and steel stretching towards the sky. I step out on shaky legs, my reflection in the polished doors barely recognizable.

I take a deep breath and step forward, the future unfolding before me like a blank page, waiting to be written. My eyes drift to the gift bag in my hand, and I can't help but grin. It's silly and maybe a little bold, but the thought of Jack's reaction sends a thrill through me.

A man exits the building, and I mutter a quick thanks as I slip inside. The elevator ride to the third floor is both too long and far too short. With each floor, my nerves ratchet up another notch. I fidget with the hem of my dress, second-guessing every decision that led me here.

Finally, I find myself staring at apartment 3B, my palms sweaty and my mouth dry. This is it. Jack's door. I could still turn back and pretend this never happened. The hallway seems to stretch endlessly, offering an easy escape.

No. I square my shoulders, giving myself a mental pep talk. You've come this far, Jennifer. *Don't chicken out now. You deserve happiness. You deserve to take a chance.* The words echo in my mind, drowning out the doubts that threaten to overwhelm me as I raise my hand.

Chapter 9

Jack

I sprawl on the plush leather couch, my feet dangling over the armrest, staring at the exposed brick ceiling of my loft apartment. The soft glow from the industrial-style floor lamp casts long shadows across the room, mirroring the whirlwind of thoughts in my mind.

It's been days since the dinner at Anna and Peter's, but I can't shake the memory of Jennifer's face—the hurt, the anger, and that flicker of something else.

My fingers drum restlessly on my thigh as I replay our conversation in the garden for the hundredth time. The vulnerability in her eyes when she admitted her fears, the way she leaned into my touch before pulling away. It took everything in me not to pull her close, to kiss away her doubts.

But I meant what I said. I'll wait. She's worth waiting for.

I sit up, running a hand through my hair, my gaze drifting to the framed photos on the industrial pipe shelving unit. Snapshots of my life—Mom and John's wedding, Honey's graduation, the kids from the youth center. But no Jennifer. Not yet.

What if she never comes? What if I've blown my chance?

I stand up, stretching my arms above my head until my back cracks. The sound echoes in the quiet apartment. I pace, my bare feet padding against the cool hardwood floors.

Jennifer's words echo in my mind, her voice soft and broken as she explained why she disappeared that night at the club.

"I saw you with her, Jack. You called her Honey."

I groan, shaking my head. Honey. Of course. My stepsister's brazen nature strikes again.

I can picture it now—Jennifer seeing Honey, all legs and attitude, sauntering up to me with that mischievous glint in her eye.

I mutter a curse under my breath, the sound echoing in the high-ceilinged space. "Damn it, Honey."

My stepsister's always had a knack for stirring up trouble, even when she's not trying.

A bitter chuckle escapes my lips as I make my way to the kitchen area. The gleaming stainless steel appliances reflect my distorted image as I reach for a glass.

Here I am, Jack Daniels, pouring myself a glass of water when what I really want is something stronger, as I'm pining after a woman who thinks I'm some kind of player because my stepsister's name is Honey.

It's like a bad joke, the kind you'd hear in a dive bar after one too many shots.

I flop back onto the couch, the leather creaking beneath me as I throw an arm over my eyes. "Christ, what a mess."

My mind drifts to the day my mom told me.

"Jack," she'd said, her voice soft. "I want you to meet someone special."

And there he was, standing in our living room—tall, distinguished, with a kind smile that reached his eyes. John

Daniels, widower and father to a spitfire of a daughter named Honey.

I snort, remembering my first thought after they got married: "Great, now I'm a walking liquor advertisement."

It wasn't until later, when the shock had worn off and I saw how happy my mom was, that I realized John was exactly what our family needed. He became the father I'd lost too young, and Honey... well, she became the pain-in-the-ass little sister I never knew I wanted.

"Jack and Honey Daniels," I mutter, shaking my head. "Sounds like a damn cocktail menu."

I can almost hear Honey's voice in my head, that familiar mix of sass and affection. "Oh, lighten up, big brother. At least we're top shelf."

A grin tugs at my lips despite myself. That's Honey for you—always ready with a quip, even in my imagination.

I shake my head, a rueful smile playing on my lips. But the amusement fades as quickly as it came, replaced by a gnawing ache in my chest. None of this matters if Jennifer won't give me a chance.

I sit up, suddenly restless. I need to do something, anything, to get out of my own head. Maybe I should call Honey and ask her to talk to Jennifer. But no, that would probably make things worse. Honey's not exactly known for her tact.

I walk over to the window, watching the city bustle below. Jennifer and I—we're both damaged goods. Scared of what we feel, of what we could be. But maybe that's not such a bad thing. Maybe it means we'll fight harder for what we have.

If we have anything at all.

My forehead rests against the cool glass, my breath fogging up the pane. I close my eyes, remembering the way

Jennifer looked at me during dinner. There was a moment, just a fleeting second, when our eyes met across the table. The candlelight flickered in her hazel eyes, and I saw a mix of emotions there—anger, hurt, but also a hint of longing. It was like she was fighting against herself, wanting to believe in me but too scared to take the risk.

The memory shifts.

Suddenly I'm back in Anna and Peter's garden, the cool night air nipping at my skin. Jennifer's voice, soft and vulnerable, echoes in my mind:

"I'm scared," she had whispered, her eyes glistening with unshed tears. "I'm scared of letting someone in again, of being vulnerable. What if I'm wrong about you?"

The raw honesty in her voice had hit me like a punch to the gut. I wanted nothing more than to wrap her in my arms, to promise her that I'd never hurt her. But I knew that words alone wouldn't be enough. Not for Jennifer.

I open my eyes, the weight of her fear settling on my shoulders. I understand her hesitation, her need to protect herself. Hell, I've been there myself.

We're both walking wounded, carrying the scars of past betrayals. But where I see a chance for healing, for something real and lasting, Jennifer sees a risk. A threat to the careful life she's rebuilt.

I run a hand through my hair, frustration and determination warring within me. I need to find a way to show her that what we have is worth the risk—that I'm not Felix, or any other man who's hurt her in the past. That I'm here, I'm real, and I'm not going anywhere.

But how do I prove this to her?

I push away from the window, my fingers raking through my hair for the umpteenth time tonight. I'm sure I look a mess, but who's here to see?

I stride across the room, past the sleek kitchen island and the unused dining table, my fingers itching to grab my phone from where it sits on the brushed metal coffee table. To call Peter and beg for her number. Just to hear her voice, to know she's okay.

But I promised her space and time. I've got to let her come to me when she's ready.

But what if she's never ready?

A sharp knock on the door jolts me from my spiral, the sound echoing off the high ceilings.

Who could it be?

The sharp rap on the door comes again, more insistent this time.

"Coming, coming," I mutter, running a hand through my disheveled hair. It's probably Honey, to complain about her latest boy drama. As much as I love my stepsister, I'm not in the mood for her antics tonight.

I reach for the doorknob, already preparing my lecture. "Honey, I swear to God if you're here to—"

The words die on my lips as I yank the door open.

Chapter 10

Jennifer

The door swings open, and Jack's voice fills the air before his eyes even find me. "Honey, I swear to God if you're here to—"

He freezes, mouth agape, eyes widening in shock. I drink him in, my body humming at the sight. He's barefoot, wearing well-worn jeans that hang low on his hips and a soft gray t-shirt that clings to his chest. His hair is deliciously mussed, like he's been running his fingers through it. For a moment, we're both frozen, the air between us crackling with electricity and unspoken words.

I swallow hard, willing my voice not to shake. "I heard you were being all broody and noble," I quip, aiming for nonchalance. "Thought I'd come see if the rumors were true."

My heart pounds, waiting for his reaction. He hasn't slammed the door in my face. That's something, right?

Jack blinks, then a slow smile spreads across his face. He quirks an eyebrow, his voice low and rough. "Want to come in and find out?"

After a nod, I step inside and find his space is sleek and modern, with clean lines and muted tones, but the touches of rustic charm—a worn leather armchair, a weathered wood coffee table—lend an air of lived-in comfort.

The sound of the door clicking shut startles me, causing my heart to race. I turn to face him, and I can't help but take in every subtle change in his expression: the tension in his jaw, the restless tapping of his fingers against his dark denim jeans.

My mind wanders, picturing his confident hands on my bare skin and his smooth voice whispering dirty promises into my ear.

"Can I get you a drink?" he asks, his voice low and inviting.

I clear my throat, trying to regain my composure. "Actually, I brought you something." I hold out the gift bag, my fingers trembling slightly as I pass it to him.

His eyes sparkle with curiosity as he takes it from me.

"Hmm, let me guess. A fruitcake? A reindeer sweater?" he teases.

Suddenly feeling exposed, I whisper, my cheeks flushing with heat. "It's my, um, my favorite drink."

He pulls out the bottle of Jack Daniels, barking out a laugh that reverberates through the room. But then he pulls out the red silk tie, and the air between us charges with electricity. His eyes meet mine, dark and questioning. "And this?"

I take a deep breath, gathering every ounce of courage I possess and diving headfirst into the deep end, my heart pounding so loudly I'm sure he can hear it.

"Well," I say, my voice huskier than I intended, "being tied up on Boxing day is on my Christmas wish list. I'm looking for someone to make those wishes come true."

He sets the bottle down with care on the nearby table, then stalks towards me, the tie dangling from his fingers like a promise of things to come. He stops mere inches away, close enough that I can feel the heat emanating from his body and smell the faint scent of cologne.

"Truth or dare, Jennifer?"

I meet his gaze, unflinching. "Truth."

"Do you trust me?"

The question hangs between us, loaded with meaning.

I take a shaky breath. "I do."

His eyes soften, and he nods. "Good."

"Last question," he murmurs. "Are you going to run away from me again?"

A small smile tugs at my lips. I shake my head, holding his gaze. "I'm not a runner, Jack. Besides," I lean in, dropping my voice to a playful whisper, "where else on Christmas can I find this level of... satisfaction?"

His pupils dilate, and a soft groan escapes his lips. "Nowhere, you've come to the right address."

I smile. "Truth or dare, Jack?"

He smirks, not missing a beat. "Truth."

"What's on top of your naughty Christmas list?"

His eyes darken, and he leans in, his voice a husky growl. "You. All of you. Naked, except for those fucking heels you're wearing."

Every nerve ending in my body tingles, and all my worries and all my fears dissolve into nothing, like mist in the morning sun. I step closer, pressing myself onto my toes before kissing him with a hunger I didn't know I possessed. His lips are soft yet firm, a perfect contradiction, and I melt into him, wrapping my arms around his neck and pulling him closer. God, I've missed the intoxicating taste of him, the solid feel of his body against mine, the way his muscles tense and relax in response to my touch.

He groans, a primal sound that reverberates through me, and as he deepens the kiss, his tongue explores my mouth with an intensity that makes my body sing and my toes curl.

Suddenly, an idea sparks in my mind, wild and daring. I break the kiss, breathless and dizzy with desire, and grab the silken tie from his hands.

"Trust me?" I ask, my voice husky with want.

His eyes darken, and he smirks that devastatingly sexy smirk of his. "Always, Princess."

That nickname again—it sends a thrill through me every time he says it. I love it more than I care to admit. With trembling fingers, I guide his hands behind his back and wrap the silk tie around his wrists, the smooth material sliding against his skin.

"I'm not a pro at this," I murmur, my fingers fumbling with the material, a mix of nervousness and excitement coursing through me. "But I want you to feel what you made me feel that night. I want to drive you wild."

When his hands are secured behind his back, I step back, admiring my handiwork. And I must say that I like the sight of him, powerful yet vulnerable, completely at my mercy.

I've never done anything like this before, never taken control like this. It's terrifying and thrilling all at once. The power I feel, the trust he's placing in me, it's intoxicating. I can feel my inhibitions evaporating and giving way to a strong desire to explore this new dynamic between us.

I wander to his front, my heart pounding in my chest as I let my hands roam over his body. Starting at his shoulders, I feel the tension in his muscles beneath his shirt. Slowly, I trace my fingers down his chest, feeling the defined lines and the warmth of his skin through the fabric. His heartbeat matches mine, strong and steady.

"What are you planning, Princess?"

I lean in closer, and trail my palm down his chest,

“First,” I murmur seductively, “I'm going to undress you.”

With trembling fingertips, I unbutton his shirt, revealing more of his taut torso with each button. When I reach the last one, he's fully exposed to me. A trail of dark hair leads down from his navel, making me salivate.

Leaning down, I place a soft kiss near his heart and feel him catch his breath. “Then,” I continue, sliding lower and caressing the bulge in his pants, “I'm going to take your cock in my mouth and taste you, tease you until you beg for more.”

He moans, thrusting into my touch.

“And finally, Jack,” I whisper as I stroke up and down his length, “I'm going to ride you until you scream out my name, while I take every inch of you.”

His breathing is heavy and I can see the struggle in his eyes, the effort it takes for him to hold back. My fingers continue playing with the button of his jeans, the thrill of anticipation making my skin tingle and my heart race. Slowly, I unbutton them before finally pulling down the zipper, savoring the moment.

“You're driving me crazy,” he gasps as his hips thrust forward. I look up at him through my lashes, feeling more seductive than ever before.

“That's exactly what I want, Christmas Prince.”

His laughter turns into a moan as I finally free him from his jeans and boxers. The sight of him, hard and ready, makes my mouth go dry.

I guide him towards a lounge chair but stop him with a hand on his chest. “Not yet,” I whisper. “I want you standing.”

He raises an eyebrow at me with a smirk on his lips. “Yes, ma'am.”

The title sends a rush of pleasure through me. I've never been one for power play, but there's something intoxicating about having this strong, powerful man at my mercy. I run my hands down his sides, relishing in the way his muscles twitch under my touch.

"You know," Jack says, leaning in close. "When I get out of these bonds, I'm going to make you scream my name."

I laugh breathily, filled with anticipation. "Big words, Jack. But right now, you're all talk and no action."

His eyes flash with challenge and desire. "Untie me and I'll show you action."

I lean in close to his ear, brushing my lips against it. "Not a chance. I'm not done with you yet."

With that, I wrap my palm around his length. He's hot and hard beneath my touch, velvet over steel, and I can feel his pulse throbbing. As I stroke him, my eyes remain locked on his face, taking in every flicker of pleasure that crosses his features. His jaw clenches and his breathing hitches, each reaction fueling my confidence.

"Fuck," he hisses, his hips jerking slightly. He closes his eyes and moans, a sound that sends a wave of heat through me. "I've dreamed of this, you know. Of you, of us. Every night for the past month."

I can't help but smirk, even as my own desire throbs between my legs, echoing his need. "Must have conjured me with all that wishing," I quip, my voice laced with playful cynicism. However, there is a part of me that is flattered and delighted at the idea of Jack dreaming of me and us, together, in the depths of his mind.

I want to know more. I want to delve into his fantasies to understand the depth of his desire.

"What did you dream about, Jack?" I sink to my knees, looking up at him, his body towering over me. "Tell me all about your dirty dreams. What did we do in them?"

His eyes darken, and he takes a deep breath, as if steeling

himself for what he's about to confess. “I dreamed of you on your knees, just like this,” he begins. “I dreamed of your mouth on me, your lips wrapping around my hard cock, taking me deep.”

Unable to resist any longer, I lean forward and run my tongue along his length. He groans and tenses, but continues speaking, his words growing more passionate with each passing moment. “I dreamed of you pleasuring yourself while you sucked me. I dreamed of you moaning as I pushed deep into your wetness, begging for more.”

His words ignite a fire inside me, sending a surge of heat throughout my body. I've never been so desperate for someone's touch before. My arousal grows stronger by the second, the throbbing between my legs demanding attention.

With trembling fingers, I slide off my panties from under my dress and toss them aside onto the couch. “You can have those, too,” I whisper before taking him into my mouth.

His taste is an addictive elixir, a sinful blend of salt and musk that sets my senses ablaze. My tongue dances around his tip, reveling in the way his body responds to my touch. He's throbbing with desire, his need pulsing with every beat of his heart. I take him deeper, savoring the way he fills me and the way his breath quickens with each stroke of my tongue.

“Fuck, Princess,” he groans, his hips bucking as he begs for more. The nickname sends shivers down my spine. It's a sweet reminder of our intimate connection; unlike any other. It's our secret code, a language only we understand, and it makes me feel like the center of his world.

I can feel the desperation in his body, his urgent need for release, and it ignites a fire within me. Knowing that I have the power to bring him to the edge and keep him there, pleading for more. My own arousal grows as I feel his body tense, his breaths coming in shallow gasps as he struggles to maintain control. I pull back slightly, locking eyes with him through my long lashes, my lips still glistening with his desire.

"Tell me what you want, Jack."

In a voice that's filled with raw need and desperation, free from any restraints, he lays himself bare before me. "I need you, Jennifer. I need to be buried deep inside you, to fuck you until your sweet pussy clenches around me."

A smirk crosses my lips as I stand up slowly, my body pulsing with need, my skin flushed with heat. "You know," I purr seductively, letting my fingers trace teasing patterns along his chest. "I've thought about you a lot this past month too."

Our eyes lock once again, the intensity between us palpable. "About your hands on me, your mouth, and all of your other impressive assets." I can't help but let my fingers drift lower.

His breath hitches sharply, and a thrill of satisfaction rushes through me.

"Please, Princess," he rasps, his voice thick with desperation.

"Hmm, I don't know," I tease, letting my hand glide slowly between my thighs, brushing against the sensitive skin there. I watch his reaction carefully. "Maybe I should just take care of myself, and you can watch."

A strangled sound escapes his lips.

"No, please. I need to touch you, feel you, make you come undone." His voice is a raw plea, overflowing with insatiable desire.

I can't resist a wicked grin as I remove my hand from between my thighs and use it to stroke him gently. "Then beg for it, Jack."

His hips jerk at my touch, and his gaze burns into mine. “Please, Princess. Let me fuck you. Let me make you feel good.”

The raw emotion in his voice, the sheer desperation, undoes me completely. I can't hold back any longer. I press my body against his, our mouths crashing together in a searing, passionate kiss. He groans deeply, his hips bucking against me, the friction sending waves of desire through me. Suddenly, he pulls away, his eyes dark with intent.

“Tell me you want me to fuck you senseless.”

I repeat his words, letting them roll off my tongue like a secret. “I want you to fuck me senseless, Jack.”

Before I can react, one of his strong arms encircles me, while the other shows the silk tie dangling from his fingers as if it were a trophy. A smirk plays on his lips, and I can see the mischief and hunger in his eyes. In one swift movement, he lifts me off the ground, and I gasp, clinging to his shoulders as he carries me effortlessly to the couch.

He places me onto the cushions, the soft fabric beneath me a sharp contrast to the hard, muscular man before me.

“How did you—” I start, my eyes wide with surprise and a hint of awe.

Jack smirks, an irresistible glint in his eyes. “I'll teach you to tie a real knot if you want, Princess.”

Realization dawns on me. He was never really tied up. He gave me control; let me lead, knowing exactly what I needed. And I find it sweet and sexy as hell.

Jack's fingers find the hem of my dress, and with a swift tug, it's pulled over my head, leaving me exposed. His eyes drink me in, a hungry gaze that sets my skin on fire.

“Fuck, Jenn. You look... fucking amazing.”

Then he grins, a wicked glint in his eyes. “Want to turn the tables? Get those hands tied up again?”

I stare at him, and something about this commanding, confident side of him—the man who surprises me at every turn—is utterly alluring. I love it, the way he can ground me one moment and set me ablaze the next. "Yes," I whisper. "But I want to ride you too."

He chuckles, a deep, rumbling sound that stokes the fire burning within me.

"I like your eagerness," he says before capturing my lips in a possessive kiss. He pulls back, his intense gaze locking with mine. "We can do both. You can be tied up and ride my dick with pleasure."

My body trembles with anticipation as he ties my hands together, his touch sending sparks of arousal through me. He kisses me again, igniting a fire within me that only grows when he steps back to admire his work. "Stay right there," he commands. "I'll be right back."

I watch as he disappears into the bedroom, my heart pounding in my chest. The absence of his touch leaves me aching, my skin tingling with anticipation. I've never felt this way before—so raw and exposed, yet so utterly safe and desired. My bound hands rest against my stomach, the soft silk a constant reminder of the power exchange between us.

When Jack reappears, a small foil packet sits in his hand and I watch him tear it open, his movements deliberate and sensual. He rolls the condom down his length, his eyes never leaving mine. I bite my lip, trying to contain the moan that threatens to escape as he stalks towards me, every step purposeful, like a predator approaching its prey. But I'm no helpless victim—I'm a willing participant in this dance of desire. He stops just inches from me, close enough that I can feel the heat radiating from his body.

"You're fucking stunning," he growls, his fingers digging into my jaw with a possessive force. I melt into his touch, craving more. “Do you even realize the power you hold over me?”

Before I can respond, he drops onto the couch, spreading his legs wide. His eyes, dark and filled with primal hunger, lock onto mine. “Get on top of me.”

I obey without hesitation, drawn to him like a moth to a flame. With my hands bound, I have no choice but to rely on him for support as I straddle him. The feeling of his hard length against my entrance makes me shiver. Despite how wet and ready I am for him, each inch of penetration takes my breath away. Slowly, agonizingly slow, I lower myself onto him, reveling in the fullness and completion I feel with him inside me.

Once he's fully sheathed within me, I pause to adjust to the intensity of the sensation. Jack's breathing is heavy and his fingers dig into my hips with restraint. The tension radiating from his body only heightens the pleasure coursing through me as I set the pace.

He groans through clenched teeth. “Fuck, you feel incredible. So tight and slick for me.”

I start to move, grinding my hips against him experimentally. The friction is electric, sending sparks of ecstasy through every nerve in my body. With my hands around his neck for support, I find a rhythm that drives us both wild.

Jack's hands slide up my sides, cupping my breasts. I arch into his touch, a moan escaping my lips as his thumbs brush over my nipples. “That's it, Princess,” he encourages hoarsely, his voice thick with desire. “Ride me like you need it.”

His mouth claims one of my nipples, sucking and nipping until I'm writhing on top of him, consumed by the intoxicating sensations. “Look at you, grinding on me like a fucking animal,” he murmurs, his voice dripping with primal lust. Each word is like a lit match, fueling the inferno between us. My hips move faster, chasing that addictive friction. His hands grip my ass, his fingers digging into my flesh as he meets my every thrust with his own, driving deeper and harder.

I've never felt so desired, so connected to another person. It's as though every touch, every word, every movement is designed to take me higher, to push me further into ecstasy. Our foreheads press together, our breaths mingling and our bodies slick with sweat. The intimacy of this moment threatens to overwhelm me, but I crave more.

"Touch me, Jack," I gasp desperately, unable to suppress the primal urge coursing through me. "Touch my asshole." The words escape before I can fully process them, driven by a raw desire that consumes us both.

His grin widens, a sly promise of something wicked. "What was that, Princess? Say it again, I want to hear." His eyes glint with mischief and challenge me to reveal my desires.

With an eye roll and a sarcastic quip ready on my tongue, he nudges me playfully. But his touch ignites a fire within me, one that demands to be sated. My hips move in sync with his, his cock sliding in and out of me with each thrust, driving me wild. "Touch my ass, Jack," I demand louder and more determined this time. "Fuck me while you touch it."

He rewards me with a searing kiss, his tongue mimicking the motions of his cock inside me. As his hands explore my backside, teasing the sensitive pucker of my asshole, I can't think or breathe or do anything but feel. "Tell me how it feels," he demands in my ear, his finger teasing the rim of my tight entrance. "I want to know how I make you feel."

I struggle to find words as pleasure overwhelms me. "It's... it's fucking amazing." I shift my hips, relishing the delicious friction. “I love how you touch every part of me. Your fingers, your mouth, your... your cock.” The admission makes my cheeks flush with heat, but the words keep pouring out fueled by my insatiable desire. “One day I want your cock in my ass, Jack. I want to feel completely owned by you.”

His movements become more urgent at my confession, a low growl rumbling in his chest. “God, Jenn. You have no idea how badly I want that.” His finger presses harder against the tight rim of my ass and I gasp as sparks of pleasure-pain shoot through me. “Imagine it, Princess. My thick cock stretching your tight little ass, filling you up until you're begging for more.”

His words and touch push me closer to the edge, a tense mix of pleasure and tension. My nails rake down the nape of his neck, marking him as mine, and he hisses in response, his cock throbbing inside me. I'm so close, so fucking close.

“Say my name when you come, Jenn,” he urges as he thrusts his finger deeper inside me. And then it's too much; my body arching as wave after wave of pleasure crashes over me.

“Jack!” I scream his name repeatedly, caught in the intensity of my orgasm.

He follows suit with his own release, a primal groan of satisfaction reverberating through the room as his hips buck up while he spills inside the condom.

We cling to each other, our fingers digging into each other's skin. This encounter will leave its mark on me for days to come, but I crave it. I need it.

Jack runs his fingers down my spine, sending shivers through me. He presses hot kisses against my neck and whispers, “You're fucking incredible, Jenn.” His voice is filled with awe and satisfaction.

I can't stop the smile that spreads across my face. “Yeah? You liked that?” I tease, my voice still shaky.

His lips brush against my ear. “Princess, you just proved that even royalty can be dirty little sluts.”

My heart races at his words, a mix of sweetness and filth that make my body ache for more. I sit up, our bodies still connected, and rest my forehead against his. Our eyes lock and I see the warmth in his gaze, a tenderness that contrasts with the roughness of our encounter.

“Looks like dreams do come true,” I whisper, my voice filled with awe. “Who knew I'd have my own Christmas Prince... one who makes me feel so alive, so free, so... seen.”

His gaze sends shivers down my spine and ignites a fire in my core. His firm grasp on my hips leaves me eager for more. “I'll give you more than just gifts this Christmas,” he whispers, his hot breath tickling my ear.

A giggle escapes my lips, laced with desire. “Is that a promise?” I taunt, already succumbing to his touch and words.

“Fuck yeah,” he murmurs before capturing my mouth in a passionate kiss. When he pulls back, his eyes bore into mine with unwavering intensity. “I'm going to make every day feel like Christmas for you, Jenn. Every. Fucking. Day.”

A surge of excitement rushes through me, transcending physical pleasure. It’s a pledge, a dedication—something I’ve been longing for but too scared to believe in.

Love can be a cruel game, but with Jack by my side, I'm starting to believe it can be something different. Something real.

I feel it, warmth spreading from my heart outward. It's trust, hope. A belief that whatever is between us is genuine and worth fighting for.

I press my lips to his again, sealing our new truth. When I

pull back, I can't help but grin, unshed tears in my eyes. "You know what, Jack?" I say confidently.

He raises an eyebrow in anticipation.

"I'm holding you to that promise."

With those words, I commit myself to him and this exhilarating journey we're embarking on together. Despite the unknowns and risks, I'm all in. For the first time in a long time, I'm not afraid. I'm alive. And most importantly, I'm in love.

Chapter 11

Epilogue

O*ne Year Later*

I wake to the scent of pine and cinnamon, a smile already tugging at my lips before I even open my eyes. Jack's arm is draped over my waist, his breath warm against my neck. For a moment, I just lie there, savoring the peace.

Then I remember what day it is.

I bolt upright, nearly knocking Jack off the bed. "It's Christmas!"

Jack groans, reaching for me. "Five more minutes, Princess."

"Not a chance, Christmas Prince," I tease, dodging his grasp. "We've got a tree to decorate!"

An hour later, we're standing in our living room, surrounded by boxes of ornaments and tangled strings of lights. The seven-foot Douglas fir we picked out yesterday towers over us, filling the room with its fresh, woodsy scent.

"Ready?" Jack asks, holding up the first string of lights.

I nod, grinning. “Let's do this.”

What follows is a whirlwind of activity. We weave lights through branches, hang glittering ornaments, and playfully argue over the perfect placement of each bauble. Jack lifts me to reach the higher branches, his hands lingering on my waist longer than necessary. I retaliate by “accidentally” brushing against him as I pass, enjoying the way his eyes darken with each touch.

As I hang the last ornament, a delicate glass snowflake, Jack wraps his arms around me from behind. “Look at us,” he murmurs, his chin resting on my shoulder. “Who would've thought we'd be here a year ago?”

I lean back into him, my heart swelling with emotion. “Certainly not cynical old me.”

He chuckles, the sound rumbling through his chest. “You've come a long way, Princess.”

And I have. The woman I was last Christmas would hardly recognize me now. I'm more open, more willing to take risks. I've learned to trust not just Jack, but myself.

“We both have,” I say, turning in his arms to face him. “Remember our first Christmas together? When I showed up at your door with a bottle of Jack and a silk tie?”

His eyes darken at the memory. “How could I forget? Best Christmas gift ever.”

I laugh, swatting his chest playfully. “Well, I hope this year's gift can live up to that.”

Jack's eyebrows shoot up. “Oh? And what might that be?”

With a grin, I break away from him and hurry to the bedroom. When I return, I'm holding a small, gift-wrapped box.

Jack takes it, curiosity written all over his face. As he unwraps it, I hold my breath, suddenly nervous. Inside is a custom-made Christmas ornament. It's a miniature replica of the club where we first met, complete with tiny flashing lights and minuscule Jack and Jennifer figures dancing inside.

He looks up at me, his eyes wide with wonder. "Jenn, this is..."

I take a deep breath. "Turn it over."

On the back, engraved in small letters, are the words: *Thank you for making every day feel like Christmas. Here's to a lifetime of adventures together.*

Jack's eyes mist over as he reads the inscription.

"But wait," I say, reaching into my pocket. "There's more."

I pull out a small, badly wrapped package. Jack raises an eyebrow. "Did you wrap this one yourself?"

I stick my tongue out at him. "Maybe. Just open it, smartass."

Inside is a red silk tie, identical to the one from our first night together. Jack's eyes darken with recognition and desire. "Is this what I think it is?"

I grin mischievously. "Well, if you're going to be my Christmas Prince all year round, I figured we needed to keep some traditions alive."

Jack immediately loops the tie around his neck, leaving it untied. "How do I look?"

"Absolutely irresistible," I say, my voice low and husky. "And completely mine."

He pulls me into his arms and lifts me off the ground, the silk of the tie brushing against my skin.

"You amazing, incredible woman," he laughs, peppering my face with kisses. "I love you so damn much."

Relief and joy wash over me. "I love you too."

As he sets me down, my gaze falls on our tree. There, nestled among the new ornaments, is the kintsugi heart. Its golden cracks catch the light, reminding me of how far I've come.

"You know," I say softly, reaching out to touch the ornament. "I used to think this represented my broken heart. But now I see it differently."

Jack's hand covers mine on the ornament. "How so?"

I turn to him, smiling through the tears that have welled up in my eyes. "Now I see it as us. Two broken pieces, coming together to create something even more beautiful."

Jack's answering smile is radiant. He cups my face in his hands, his thumbs brushing away my tears. "Merry Christmas, Princess," he murmurs, before capturing my lips in a kiss that leaves me breathless.

As we break apart, a mischievous glint enters his eye. "Now, about this silk tie..."

I laugh, already backing towards the bedroom. "Race you!"

As I run, Jack hot on my heels, I can't help but marvel at how much has changed in a year. Last Christmas, I was a woman afraid to love. This Christmas, I'm racing towards it with open arms.

And I wouldn't have it any other way.

Afterword

Thank you for picking up "Wrapped Up" and diving headfirst into the magic of Jennifer and Jack's love story. I hope their tale has left you feeling breathless, giddy, and maybe even a little inspired to take a chance on love yourself.

And I can promise you, this is only the beginning. Jennifer and Jack's journey may be complete, but I have so many more captivating tales of romance, passion, and happily-ever-after waiting to be told. So stay tuned, my darlings, because the best is yet to come.

Now, I have a favor to ask—if you enjoyed this story, please leave a review on your preferred retail platform. Even a small review with just one sentence means the world to me and helps make this book visible to others. Those honest, heartfelt responses are the greatest gift you can give an author, ensuring that more stories like this one find their way into the world.

And last but not least, I'd like to give a heartfelt thank you to my incredible beta readers—your time, insight, and enthusiasm were invaluable in shaping this novella. I couldn't have done it without you.I also want to express my gratitude to my talented editors, whose keen eyes and thoughtful suggestions refined this story into what it is today.

And to my amazing cover artist—thank you for crafting a beautiful visual that perfectly captures the vibe and energy of this book, fitting Jennifer and Jack's love story beautifully. Your artistry has truly brought this book to life in ways I couldn't have imagined.

Wishing you all a very merry and romantic holiday season,

Marlyn Love

About the Author

Marlyn Love is a Dutch author who has been in love with romance novels since she first discovered them as a teenager. When she's not busy weaving tales of passion and happily-ever-after, you can find her spending quality time with her own "Christmas Prince" - her husband - and their beautiful, teenage daughter.

In her free time, Marlyn loves to get lost in a good book and simply savor all the beauty and joy that life has to offer. She is the author of the Irresistible series, novels that feature strong, female heroines and complicated, but irresistible heroes that will make you laugh, cry, and yearn for one of your own.

"Wrapped Up" is the latest addition to Marlyn's growing library of captivating romance stories. Rest assured, this won't be the last time you'll be swept away by her words and the characters that capture your heart.

Also by Marlyn Love

Simply Irresisibtle

Unbreakable Bonds

Beyond Friendship

Printed in Dunstable, United Kingdom

75183581R00067